D0231035

Published by Jolo Press

Copyright © 2004 Joan Lock
This paperback edition published 2016

Joan Lock has asserted her right
under the Copyright, Designs and Patents Act 1988
to be identified as the author of this work

ISBN 978-1-53509-735-2

Also available as a Kindle ebook

A CIP catalogue record for this
book is available from the British Library.

This is a work of fiction. Any resemblance
between the characters and situations depicted and
real life is purely coincidental.

Pre-press production
eBook Versions
27 Old Gloucester Street
London WC1N 3AX
www.ebookversions.com

Other books by Joan Lock

DEAD CENTRE

The seventh Inspector Best Mystery

Joan Lock

JOLO PRESS

1

How long can this go on, wondered Detective Inspector Earnest Best as he contemplated the extraordinary scene before him.

On the ground all across Trafalgar Square lay hundreds of sleeping people: men, women and children. Some were alone, more were huddled together for warmth. The October nights were becoming sharper now.

The luckier ones, or those who had got there early enough, or were more sensible, had found refuge in the lee of the sunken square's eastern parapet or the western walls of the fountain basins which sheltered them a little from the chill north east wind.

Best carried out his surveillance from a prudent distance. Despite her sympathies with the vermin's original hosts Helen would not thank him for coming home lice-ridden once again. He, himself, being a fastidious man, shuddered at the prospect. However, if he was obliged to make an arrest he would have no choice, lice or not.

He was relieved to see that most of the crowd had already settled down - as far as they were able in the circumstances. One tumble-haired child, about the same age as Lucy, was restless in her mother's arms. As sleep overcame the weary woman, the pair slid down from their propped-up position by the north wall.

He was about to take his leave, unsullied by lice, when he noticed a man also sitting up, his back against one of the fountain basins. Only *he* was awake, looking about him. Not yet ready for sleep? Too cold and uncomfortable? Not surprising. Or, perhaps, he had something else on his mind? The straggly-bearded face, fronted by spindly wire spectacles, seemed vaguely familiar.

Best shrugged. So many people wandered in and out of view in the life of a Scotland Yard detective. This one could be an old customer looking for an opportunity to steal from one of the slumbering forms. Well, pickings would be thin among these ragged, often shoeless folk.

Nonetheless, before he went back to the Yard to sign off, Best pointed the man out to one of the several uniformed constables engaged in keeping an eye on the crowd.

Then he made his way down to the Thames Embankment and along to Charing Cross underground station. He gave thanks, once again, that the Circle comprised by the Metropolitan and District Railways had recently been completed saving him the great trek across London to Notting Hill by several omnibuses.

He took a few deep breaths before descending into the depths and darkness with the usual late-night passengers.

They were an oddly assorted crowd: middle-class theatre goers; the working class audience from the last house at the Alhambra Music Hall in Leicester Square some of them still singing the latest songs; revellers who had revelled rather more than was sensible; top-hatted gentlemen from the St James's clubs who preferred a quick, murky underground trip to a long rattle home in a cab; prostitutes and shopkeepers having finally shut up shop. But, he fervently hoped, no pick-pockets. He didn't want to have to make an arrest. He had promised Helen that, tonight, if at all possible, he would be home around midnight.

Nevertheless, his attention was attracted to a pair of young men glancing about – with apparent innocence - as they struggled to board his second-class carriage. However, once they were on they settled down quietly by the window. Maybe Helen was right, he was becoming too cynical and suspicious.

As usual, the air was foul. It was always at its worst at this time of night the tunnels choked with the day's build-up of sulphurous, smut-laden steam.

In this instance the stench was made worse by the pungent cigar smoke issuing from the silk-hatted gentleman sitting opposite, his knees almost touching Best's. Clearly, the first class carriages were full but the man was determined to get home by train, cramped or not.

As the stations came and went: Westminster, St James's Park, Victoria ... Best's mind drifted back to the sights of the square. Ragged bodies tucked around the foot of the column supporting the statue commemorating England's greatest hero, Admiral Lord Nelson, their heads resting just below the bronze reliefs depicting four of his famous victories.

Then there was the little tumble-haired girl so like Lucy and yet not – much

2

thinner and paler, the suspicious straggly-haired man who probably wasn't suspicious at all, simply having a look around and wondering, like him, how this ridiculous situation had been allowed to develop?

It seemed to Best that this nightly annexing of Trafalgar Square by the unemployed and homeless had occurred not exactly by stealth but almost when the authorities had their backs turned - distracted by Queen Victoria's glittering Silver Jubilee celebrations and the problems of guarding her from threatened attempts to assassinate her during the revelry.

The occupation of Trafalgar Square, which stood at the very heart, the dead centre, of the world's wealthiest city, had begun several weeks earlier following fiery daytime meetings and marches demanding work and endeavouring to awake the consciences of the wealthy and the powerful.

Some of the crowd had begun to hang around the square afterwards. Then the homeless stayed the night rather than seek shelter under a bridge, in a doorway or down an alleyway or in one of the casual wards of the workhouses.

They would stay here where everyone could see them. Not conveniently out of sight and out of mind. The numbers staying for the night at the heart of the Empire kept growing until they became a great embarrassment to the authorities particularly in this celebratory year when the eyes of the world were upon them.

Best closed *his* eyes. Not to sleep but to shut out the cramped and uncomfortable surroundings. But the insistent, steady rumble of the train and the hot, dense atmosphere soon caused the weary Detective Inspector to descend into that halfway state between sleep and wakefulness. More dimly-lit stations came and went: Sloane Square, South Kensington and Gloucester Road.

Just before they arrived at High Street Kensington the day's images formed into a montage of Nelson's Column; banners held aloft; William Morris proclaiming to the crowd; the crowd's shouts in response and those of the Socialist League as they sold their magazine, The Commonweal; the huddled sleepers; Helen and Lucy at breakfast; the tumbled-haired child and the suspicious, staring man.

Suddenly, the jerky braking as they pulled into the station caused two of the images to coalesce: the child and the suspicious man. This time, the man wore a short, prison-cut hair and no spectacles.

Best's eyes flew open.

'My God! It's Stark!' Best shouted, to the astonishment of the other passengers.

'It's Stark!' he repeated as he shot to his feet and pushed his way through the tangle of legs to the accompaniment of curses and exclamations about the madmen that were allowed to roam freely among them these days.

He wrenched open the door and leaped out onto the platform just as the guard was signalling the train's departure. He was not going to reach home around midnight after all.

2

The blackness was almost total. Florence could only sense the tall buildings she knew loomed sinisterly on either side of her.

She moved carefully, aware that if she stumbled over one of the rocky paving stones or fell into one of the ragged holes she might sprain her ankle again or drop her precious burden.

She tried to ignore the occasional ominous squelching underfoot as she stepped into who knew what filth, to shut out the sudden scuttling sounds and foul smells and not to think about predators who could be lurking in this alley into which even lone policemen hesitated to venture. She had to go on. *She* had no choice. It was her duty.

As her eyes gradually became more accustomed to the darkness she caught a glimpse of a familiar hovel to her left. Then, to her relief, the heavy cloud obscuring the moon drew back to reveal the very place she was seeking: 17, Rye Court. She had several calls to make in this tenement.

After climbing to the first floor she stopped outside second door to the left, gave a gentle knock and went in.

On a pile of clothes in the far corner of the room lay five year-old Hannah who suffered from some nameless illness which Florence suspected might be tuberculosis. Two more sickly-looking children were hunched over the fireplace trying to warm themselves at the meagre, near-dead coals.

Lizzie Carter was in her usual place, sitting at a table, baby strapped to her chest with a threadbare shawl, and doing the usual thing - making silk flowers for which she earned six shillings for five dozen.

Florence had thought this not too mean a reward until she learned that Lizzie was obliged to fork out four shillings for the materials and that, should any of the resulting flowers be deemed to be less than perfect, would have money docked from the remaining two shillings.

Lizzie usually looked up from her work and gave the young Salvation Army lass a welcoming smile but on this occasion did not turn her head. Florence guessed why. She did not approach her, just called out a cheery hello then went over to each child in turn, handed them a lump of bread and cheese and a toffee. Her circular tour ended directly opposite Lizzie who kept her head bent to her task still refusing to look up.

'Let me put something on that eye,' Florence murmured casually, and reached for her satchel.

Lizzie's head shot up.

'Oh no! No!' She looked towards the door fearfully. 'He'd know I'd seen you and . . .' She shook her head frantically, wincing with pain as she did so.

'Have a little break then.'

Florence sat down, pushed a sandwich over to Lizzie and picked up some of the rose-coloured silk petals, 'I'll make a few for you.'

Lizzie nodded dumbly but seemed unable to stop her hands from automatically picking up several glossy petals, closing them around a stamen and a stalk, winding wire around to hold them together, then reaching out again.

Florence closed her hands over Lizzie's, held them still and nodded towards the food. 'I know I'm not as quick or neat as you,' she laughed, 'but I am improving and wont spoil any, I promise.'

Lizzie stared down at her fingers for a moment then up at Florence who knew better than offer sympathy. In her experience nothing could more easily undo a person who was in a low state than a show of kindness. She sometimes had difficulty trying to impress that fact upon new recruits who were eager to show they cared but did not realise how much damage their sympathy could do.

They sat quietly. Florence tried to stop the silk from slipping from her fingers as she bound the petals together. Lizzie made an effort to nibble at the bread and cheese through swollen lips while gazing numbly into the distance.

'You know you can come to us whenever you like?' murmured Florence without raising her eyes from the pretty pink rose she was doing her best to perfect.

Lizzie shook her head, more slowly this time, gesturing towards the children. 'It's no good. He said he'd kill us all if I tried to leave.'

Florence inclined her head in rueful acknowledgement of the difficulty but continued, 'We'd do our best to protect you. We could send you away.'

She knew it would be foolish to swear they could guarantee their safety. Angry husbands had ways of finding runaway wives but she suspected that if Lizzie didn't get away soon Jake Carter would kill them all anyway.

Joe Benbow would never have hurt his waiflike wife. He watched Elsa constantly, concern in his eyes, while she tried to drink the soup Florence had brought. In her case, the effort was not due to bruised and swollen lips but weakness from having arisen too soon after the difficult birth of a baby boy, now dead.

The physical contrast between the pair could not have been more pronounced. Elsa was fair, pale and fragile, looked hardly more than a child. Joe, with his bull-like neck and shoulders made solid from gruelling physical work loading and unloading the ships. His thick black hair was cropped short and his dark eyes brimmed with a latent anger reminding Florence of her father's intense gaze although the reasons for their intensity were very different. She shuddered and pushed the memory away.

'She went out trying to sell our pans,' Joe exclaimed. 'I told her not to!'

Elsa looked at him sadly then nodded towards their twin boys sitting silently on the floor together with their backs against the wall of their mean little room.

'They were hungry,' she said simply and extended her hands in explanation.

Florence did not enquire whether Joe had managed to get any work at the docks that day. The answer was obvious. He had not. The workhouse they were so anxiously trying to avoid loomed larger. If *he* killed his family it would be out of pity and desperation. It happened quite often.

'I stayed on, hoping another ship might blow in but it didn't,' he said, clearly anxious she should not think he had neglected Elsa, 'Not enough wind in the right direction.'

Florence had witnessed the degrading spectacle of dockers fighting for a day's work and also the sad rows of men having failed to be selected for work by the caller-on, hanging about in hope, 'just in case'.

Sometimes another ship did come in. But even then there would be the same desperate struggle to catch the foreman's eye.

Out in the murky street again Florence began to feel weary – in spirit as well as body. Her night's work had begun with the usual four hours duty on the steps of the East London Hospital and at theatre doors trying to persuade young women bedizened with paint and decked out with Birmingham jewellery to stop selling their bodies and accompany her to their rescue home instead.

She smiled to herself. That, she supposed, was the Gutter part of the work of the Salvation Army's Cellar, Gutter and Garrett Brigade. She realised that their aim was to take the devil by the throat and shake him she did sometimes wonder whether the title of her particular brigade was just a little too blunt.

She shivered. The night was getting chillier. She should have worn her cape but it looked quite smart and warm and sometimes that embarrassed her when faced with such poorly and inadequately dressed people. The cape also somehow made her seem more official which men, she noticed, particularly, did not like. They could become aggressive at the mere sight of her.

Her step quickened. Only two more visits and they should not prove too depressing. Sometimes she felt her heart would break at the pity of it all.

At least she did not need food for these final calls. Just how much she and her fellow CGG members should take from their own mouths to give to the needy was a constant problem. They wanted to give everything they had but knew if they gave too much they would become weak and fall ill and so not be able to help others.

Florence approached her next call glowing with hope and barely suppressed excitement. Jenny Pomfrey had seen the light. Was almost saved. Was about, Florence was certain, to accept the Lord into her life.

When Florence first met pretty little Jenny she had sworn that she was quite happy with her life just as it was, thank you. She had absolutely no desire to cease drinking and soliciting prostitution – the latter largely to provide for the former. She certainly did not want to be 'saved'. Indeed, she had greeted the proposition with loud and raucous laughter. She had seen what a terrible thing it was to work for a living in the sweat shops around here and there was nothing else for the likes of her.

Then she had fallen ill. Florence had nursed her, become close to her, learned her sad story and, eventually heard admit that she was, in truth, not at all happy with the way her life had turned out. In fact, she was miserable and despairing.

While ill, Jenny had been unable to drink alcohol. It had made her sick. Florence had seized the opportunity offered by this involuntary abstemiousness to encourage her to stay sober afterwards, propping her up while she did so.

Inevitably, there had been some falls from grace but gradually, wanting to please Florence, Jenny became a different person. Florence had pointed out that pleasing God was a more desirable goal but so far had not been heeded.

Though uneducated, Jenny was a bright, sharp and funny girl who made

Florence laugh, sometimes guiltily, when she seized her bonnet, clamped it to her head and marched up and down enthusiastically banging an imaginary tambourine, guying the performance of the 'Hallelujah Lasses' at street corner meetings just like they did at the music halls. She began to realise how much she looked forward to seeing this wayward young girl – saved or not.

Undoubtedly, there was still a way to go. But Jenny had finally agreed that tonight, this very night, she would come with Florence to the Salvation Army Rescue Home 'just to have a look'.

She was not aware of extent of Florence's expectations. That she hoped that the young prostitute would eventually give herself to the Lord and become a cadet in the Salvation Army training school.

Once there, she would learn about their work, take bible classes, join in their marches and meetings with as much enthusiasm as she had shown in her pretend performances.

She would graduate to going out selling *The War Cry* and *The Little Soldier* in pubs and hospitals, do duty with the London Slum Corps and Prison Gate Brigade and eventually, when she had become an officer, even work alongside Florence in the Cellar, Gutter and Garrett Brigade.

What a day that would be! A triumph for the Lord.

Florence smiled to herself at the thought. On that day, she thought, she could be forgiven if she indulged, just a little, in the sin of pride.

By this time of night Jenny was usually soliciting outside The Pavilion Theatre in Whitechapel High Street catching the customers coming out after the performance ended. Florence had begged her to stop going now that she was sober most of the time.

'But I've got to eat!' she had exclaimed and then added wickedly, 'anyway it's something to do, innit?'

She would certainly have plenty to do after tonight if she kept her promise and Florence was sure she would. She had told her so over and over again. In fact, she had sworn on her own life.

Unlike many East End prostitutes, Jenny did not live in a Common Lodging houses where, for 8d a night, she could have rented a double bed for herself and her 'husband'. The keepers, their palms greased, tended not to notice that the husband changed several times in a night or that their lust seemed unbounded.

No, Jenny had the luxury of a whole room to herself. This was partly because she was so pretty and appealing and therefore better than many at attracting customers. Even when tipsy there was something irresistible about that knowing grin.

Her tiny, bleak and bare room was on the second floor back of a dilapidated three-story house in a festering alleyway. For the privilege of staying there she paid two shillings a week although she had confided to Florence that the rent should be four shillings.

'But,' she had said with a wink, ' 'e gives me a reduction cos I smile at 'im nicely.'

Florence had no illusions about 'the smile' but comforted herself that Jenny would soon be putting it to better use in the service of the Lord.

She turned into the doorway and, with her free hand, began to push open the heavy door. Suddenly, it was jerked back violently and a tall, dark figure hurtled out, collided with her and knocked her bonnet askew. She swayed, almost dropping her bag and satchel.

The man swore at her in some foreign tongue and hurried away without looking back.

Shaking, she pulled herself up, straightened her bonnet, took a deep breath and began to climb the stairs. They were lit only by a faintly-flickering oil lamp, set in the wall, which threatened to die out any minute leaving her blind and stumbling.

As she ascended she became aware of how quiet the house seemed tonight. No wailing child, no drunken altercations or doors slamming in anger.

The silence was almost eerie, unsettling. Was everyone out? If so, where? Was something happening that she didn't know about?

Perhaps, Florence thought fancifully, the neighbours intuitively realised that this was a special time heralding a new life for one of them and were showing due respect. She had noticed that despite all the violence and deprivation in their own lives most of the poor were kind to each other.

She also noticed that the banister was as rickety as ever. It had a nasty habit of suddenly jolting sideways and threatening to make her lose her balance and tumble ignominiously downstairs as she had done on one occasion. She steadied herself by placing her left hand on the wall and reached the top with her dignity and her ankle still in tact.

As she paused, breathless, on the landing she was surprised to see Jenny's door was open. She knocked and called out, always aware that privacy was just as precious to the poor as to the wealthy, particularly to those who struggled so hard to keep out of Common Lodging Houses or, God forbid, the workhouse.

Of course it was possible, and the thought made her spirits sink, that Jenny might be with a customer. She could have forgotten her promise or be drunk.

Florence called out again, hesitated, giving anyone inside time to make themselves respectable. Then she went in.

3

Best drummed his fingers on his knee in frantic frustration. Why was it taking so long? If only there was some quick way of warning people!

Why hadn't he recognised Stark at once? If only he had. He couldn't bear to think of the possible consequences of his memory lapse. It compounded his first mistake when he had let the man escape. He should have anticipated that foot thrust in his path that night in Rye Court.

They were stopping again. What station was this? He stared out of the carriage window but couldn't see the name. The lighting was so dim and they all looked alike. If you did not keep count of the stops it was easy to miss yours.

As usual, the train only halted for what seemed seconds. What if *he* should overshoot now? Time was vital. *Didn't they realise time was vital!*

Yet again he wished that he hadn't gone down to Whitechapel that evening in search of long-firm-swindler, Archie Baxter. Had he gone on another night he would not have seen those terrible sights in Rye Court nor been obliged to follow up the case because the local DI was too busy chasing some Fenian bent on killing the Queen.

Abruptly, with a screeching of wheels, metal on metal, the train came to a grinding halt. One passenger groaned in recognition of the familiar problem. Others just sighed and exchanged rueful glances.

When this happened Best usually glanced about him to check whether there was some elderly person present who might be overcome by the build up of smoke and steam in the tunnels or a timorous young lady threatening to faint.

Now he could scarcely restrain himself from struggling through the forest of knees to the door, jumping off the train and running along the track to get back to Trafalgar Square in time. He closed his eyes and prayed hoping God would forgive this lapsed Catholic and hear him.

The strain must have shown. The man opposite Best suddenly leaned forward, tapped him on the knee, smiled and said, 'I expect she'll wait for you.'

Best managed a half smile and a nod, his good manners momentarily overriding his irritation and frustration.

A hissing and rattling heralded a resumption of their journey. The next stop was his at last: Charing Cross Station! Best pushed his way out of the compartment to a chorus of complaints about the bad manners of some people today, dashed along the platform, up the stairs and into Villiers Street. At the Western end of The Strand he turned left towards Trafalgar Square.

Once there he hurried straight to the spot where he had last seen Stark. He stood there, staring about him, while trying to get his breath back. But, of course, there was no sign of the man.

Best began striding through the sleeping throng, peering closely at several male figures, even uncovering the faces of some or turning them over so he could see their features.

This did not prove popular.

'Wot d'you want, mate? Bugger orf!'

'For Christ's give us a bit of peace, won't you!'

Then his eyes lit upon a male figure huddled at the foot of the north wall. He caught his breath. The man was rolled almost into a ball as if trying to hide himself from view but Best saw a straggly beard peeping out from under a brown woollen hat which had been pulled right down! His spirits rose. Got him!

He hurried over, shook the man hard.

'Come on! Wake up! Wake up!'

But as he unrolled Best saw that he was older than Stark and, when he opened his mouth to curse at this rude awakening, he displayed only two upper and one lower tooth. Stark had a full set. Best had reason to know that. He had seen the bite marks the man had left.

Disconsolate, Best apologised and pressed a coin into the man's grimy hand.

Stark had escaped again. There was no sign of that evil man.

'You must stop blaming yourself,' Helen insisted as she pulled her dressing gown more tightly around her. 'It wasn't your fault that he escaped.'

'Yes, but I should have *recognised* him. I'm supposed to, I'm a policeman! Why didn't I?'

'Because he looked different. He was in a place you didn't expect to see him. You were tired and it was dark. You know all this, Earnest, and you know you're not infallible. No-one is.'

It had been ten past four when he finally got home but she had woken up the instant he came in and had come downstairs to greet him, make him a drink and a sandwich.

Now, she patted his hand. 'At least you know he is still about and what he looks like now. That means you can tell your colleagues and warn people.'

'If it's not too late!'

'Stop it, Earnest. *You're* supposed to be the optimist in this household.'

He shrugged. 'Not any more.'

'Yes you are. I insist. It's one of the reasons I married you, to cheer me up.' She smiled at him. 'And you know that the things we dread happening most rarely do. It's the sneaky little things which creep up behind us when we are not looking which explode and cause us grief.'

'Thank you Samuel Smiles,' he grinned ruefully, 'that's really cheered me up. Now I'll be forever looking over my shoulder expecting the worst!'

'No you won't.' She laughed and kissed him on the forehead. 'You're too sensible for that.'

He grinned again, this time more cheerfully and pulled her onto his lap. 'You're right. Now, help me to keep my mind off that man.'

She did. But later, when he turned over for sleep scenes from that awful night in Whitechapel kept coming back into his head.

It was a cold, still night with no breeze to help disperse the noxious smells of the neighbourhood and Rye Court was ominously quiet.

He had been told by the local coppers that strangers were not welcome here. Were treated with suspicion even if not suspected of being police officers. He also knew that news of his quest could have gone before him.

Perhaps he should have waited until daylight. But he had wanted to get this long-firm business over with. He did not want to have to come all the way down here again tomorrow. In any case, he was anxious to catch Archie Baxter as soon as possible. His frauds had done such damage to struggling tradesmen even causing one of them to commit suicide. He wanted to face the perpetrator with the results of his deeds even though he would probably not give a damn.

He had become used to some of the awful sights seen by police officers and the constant lies told to them even when it was not necessary but not the sheer callousness of some perpetrators.

He peered one by one at the house numbers. The one he was looking for must be at the far end of the alley. He was almost there when a piercing, bloodcurdling scream cut through the wall of silence. As far as he could tell it came from an upper room just ahead on his left. Another scream followed, then two shorter, more pathetic bleats.

Then it was all silence again apart from the pounding of his own footsteps as he ran towards the house. Violence, particularly against women, was common around here. The assaults on them, mainly committed by their husbands or lovers, rarely resulted in arrests.

This was not his manor. But he was here and had to do something. As he ran he realised that the screams had not really sounded like those of a woman taking a beating, pleading for mercy. More like one in a state of sudden fright, terror and disbelief.

As he reached the door a tiny, terrified figure came hurtling out. A figure in the uniform of the Salvation Army.

Best had never seen a Hallelujah Lass run, even when being pelted with rubbish and stones while on one of their parades, nor when venturing into dark alleys like this. Truth was that poor people around here respected them for their bravery and good deeds and would often protect them rather than abuse them. But not always.

Later that day Best was back at Trafalgar Square keeping an eye open for pickpockets and trouble-makers aiming to stir up the crowd to run riot as they had last year. He had volunteered for the duty usually left to the lower ranks, so that he could resume his search for Stark.

From late afternoon he watched the comings and goings in the square but saw no sign of the man. He was pleased to find that one of the uniformed constables on duty was Albert Roberts, a handsome and muscular young Cornishman who had an even stronger interest in seeing Stark captured.

Albert was the fiancé of Florence Bagnall the terrified Sally Army girl who had cannoned into Best that evening in Rye Court back in March.

On their first meeting Albert had become her saviour and hero when a gang of roughs had attacked their parade. Ever since, he had worried constantly about Florence's safety.

Best thought that he must at least be relieved that the man had been seen in the Square last night rather then down in Whitechapel where Florence worked.

The minute he saw Best he hastened over exclaiming without preamble, 'I hear Stark was in the square last night! What do you think it means? What was he doing?'

Best shook his head. 'I've no idea. I've been trying to fathom it out but apart from,' he paused, 'apart from . . .'

'Looking for more victims?' Albert finished for him.

Best inclined his head ruefully at the anxious young man then described as much as he could remember about Stark's present appearance. He felt embarrassed that he could not recall more. He could not shake off the feeling that there *was* more lurking in the back of his mind but refusing to come forward.

Suddenly, in the way of these things, it did. 'There *was* something else!' he exclaimed. Why did the memory do that sometimes, he wondered? Hold back information like the most reluctant witness? 'He was limping,' Best said. 'Putting all the weight on his right leg. That's it. He was limping.'

They gazed around at the crowd now settling down again for the night. Some were grateful recipients of a little food or a blanket brought by sympathisers. Only a few were still moving around searching for friends or seeking out a more sheltered position.

Friendships and alliances were being formed in this open-air bedroom. Some dangerous, Best suspected. But he saw no-one resembling Stark, limp or no.

Albert sighed. 'What am I going to do about Florence?'

Albert Roberts was a friendly, likeable fellow who shared everything and that included his troubles, real or imagined. He would present the dilemmas to friends and colleagues hoping for a solution even though, as in this case, he knew there wasn't any. He was quite aware that he could not stop Florence doing her rounds armed only with the protection of the Lord but somehow seemed to gain comfort by being reassured that this was so.

'*I* can't look after her when I'm working a twelve hour day here!'

'You can only warn her of the dangers,' Best agreed, 'keep an eagle eye out for Stark – and pray.' How, he wondered, did this lad cope with all the lone decisions constantly required of a policeman out on the streets? Perhaps he acted differently when it wasn't personal.

'But,' Albert started.

He got no further as, just then, a portly, balding little man with a red face, steel half-spectacles and a hastily-donned overcoat on top of his shopkeepers' linen jacket, marched up to him and almost shouted.

'When is this going to *stop*! They're ruining my business!' He pointed across to a row of shops in Cockspur Street which led off the south west corner of the square. 'They're ruining *all* our businesses! They keep telling us the rabble will soon be cleared away. But they never *are*! They soon would be if they occupied

Carlton House Terrace! It would be different then!'

He was babbling now, all his anger and frustration spilling out.

'Respectable people won't come here any more. Just sightseers and these – they're not the unemployed – you *know* most of them are not. They're just the usual verminous workhouse loafers. Look at them! Look at them! Most of them don't even *want* to work!'

His verbal torrent was interrupted by shouts from just below one of the four couchant bronze lions which guarded the foot of Nelson's column. Frantically-waving arms beckoned them. The man could have been taking a quiet nap sitting up as he was in a niche formed by the corner of the plinth supporting the lion. But it was quite clear that he was dead and had been for some time.

Not only was he immobile and very obviously not breathing. His skin was a waxen blue-grey colour and his lips and fingernails pale and cold. No sign of rigor yet though.

'He's got my place,' complained a filthy and gnarled old man. 'I *always* sleep there. It protects me from the wind – I've got arthritis - and it keeps other people off me.'

Best imagined that not many people would want to be near the filthy old man but he just nodded.

'He wasn't shifting so I just give him a nudge but he didn't wake up, did he?' the old man complained between wheezes. The corpse was clearly being inconsiderate. Deliberately obstructive in fact.

Neither of the two police officers were particularly shocked to find a dead man among the living like that. It was quite common to come across one amongst people who were sleeping on the streets; victims of cold, hunger or disease, their wasted bodies finally acquiescing to the inevitable.

But this man was different. There was none of that rancid unwashed smell. His skin and hair were not grimy and lank with the dirt nor his face pinched and hollowed. Indeed his broad, fleshy cheeks had the look of someone adequately fed and his dark brown hair was clean and springy. Though beardless, he sported long sideburns and his brown eyes were wide open - as if he had been startled when the grim reaper had suddenly reached out for him.

It was obvious to Best that this was not one of the unemployed but neither were his clothes and adornments of the first quality or high fashion such as might be worn by a wealthy man who had strayed drunkenly from one the nearby gentlemen's clubs. Being a bit of a dandy himself Best had an eye for such things.

However, the man's blue serge sack-style coat, matching waistcoat and

Derby shoes suggested someone perhaps a little higher on the social scale than those aristocrats of the working class, the well-paid artisans.

The light was dim but as far as Best could see the body was not that of a young man though not an old one either. There was a scattering of white hairs among the brown and judging by the colour of his skin he worked out doors for much of his time. He was, perhaps, about forty-five-years of age.

Best sent Albert for the hand ambulance then examined the body as thoroughly as possible. But he could find no obvious injury which might account for the man's sudden death. A heart attack, then? Or a stroke?

And who was he? Best went through his pockets for clues to his identity. In the right hand trouser pocket he found three pounds in silver and three pence in bronze. In the jacket and waistcoat: a pocket watch with a couple of fob attachments (a silver vesta case engraved with the initials H M and a miniature compass), a silver money clip holding two five pound notes, a brown leather diary and some kind of club membership card in a leather case.

He took the card over to the nearest lamp post. It was not the membership card of a private club nor, as he had thought more likely, of the Mechanics or Civil Engineers Institute.

Writ large across the top of the card were the words LIBERTY, EQUALITY, FRATERNITY.

Below, an oak tree with swirling branches supported a plethora of leaves and acorns. Amongst them were three scrolls emblazoned with the words, EDUCATE ORGANISE AGITATE, and a banner proclaiming SOCIAL DEMOCRATIC FEDERATION.

The reverse informed Best that the holder was one Mr Andrew Myers.

'Oh, damn,' he said.

The Social Democratic Federation or SDF were the principal organisers of the Trafalgar Square meetings and marches.

While the man's death was probably a natural one *they* might not *want* to see it that way. They might look to blame the police as they were fond of doing.

'He's one of their big bugs, isn't he?' said Albert who sometimes liked to point out the obvious.

Best nodded. 'He certainly is.'

Myers might not be as well known an agitator as Henry Hyndman, John Burns, Annie Besant and William Morris but he was significant and well known for his verbal attacks on the police particularly since Black Monday.

'In that case,' Best sighed, '*I* had better do the report.'

That meant that he would be obliged to leave watching out for Stark to the eager but ill-equipped Albert Roberts who had never actually seen that dreadful man.

4

Pc Edward Armitage was a man whose cheerful demeanour was somewhat at odds with his work as a Coroner's officer which involved dealing with the problems arising from sudden deaths.

Best was pleased to see his old friend. He and Armitage had been young rookies together back in N division where their tasks had included the control of the crowds pouring into Islington's Agricultural Hall for the latest minstrel concert or livestock show.

They had also indulged in a little mischievous fun together such as hiding the mounts of those who were annoying Islington's populace with their velocipede mania. Armitage had always been one for fun.

Today, however, his manner was sober. He, too, seemed aware of the possible public and Press reactions to the sudden death of one of the more prominent SDF members.

'I've seen Mrs Myers,' he told Best 'and she insists that he didn't have heart trouble nor, come to that, any other serious condition.'

He took his pipe from his jacket pocket, still the same old battered briar, Best noticed, placed it on the desk followed by a Cope's Red Breast Flake tobacco tin which had a fat robin on the lid.

'So there has to be a post mortem to find the cause of death.'

Armitage nodded, sighed heavily, 'Yes.' He opened the tin, teased out some tobacco and began filling his pipe. 'But,' he paused holding some strands suspended in mid-air to ensure that he had Best's full attention, 'we already know what killed him.' He began tucking the tobacco in as he added, 'Well, what we *suspect* killed him.'

Best's heart sank. 'Not a deliberate act?'

Armitage grimaced ruefully, stuffed more tobacco strands into the bowl and took out his matches.

'But I didn't see any injury or blood? The light wasn't very good but...' Best frowned. 'Was he poisoned then?'

Poisoning was the vogue these days but it was usually confined to loved ones in the privacy of their own homes. The poisoning of a public figure who then died out in the open would certainly be something new.

Armitage was still too busy fussing with his pipe, tamping down and taking little experimental puffs, to reply immediately. The man had always had this irritating habit of making you drag information out of him and using his smoking ritual to this end. Best was not going to humour him by asking again.

Could it be that Myers had been poisoned when demonstrating his brotherhood with the homeless by accepting food or drink from one of those charitable folk who brought it to the square? That would be ironic. But who would want to do that to him? The man was a hero to the square's homeless although, perhaps, not to those upset by the nuisance they caused.

'Not surprising you saw no sign,' Armitage said eventually when satisfactory ignition had been achieved. 'It was only a small knife wound.' He pointed to the left side of his chest with the stem of his pipe. 'Just below the heart. A tiny slit. They nearly missed it when he was on the slab. And it bled only a little into the lining of his waistcoat.'

'Oh, damnation,' Best exclaimed. 'Does the Commissioner know yet?'

'No. Just going to see him. Thought I'd warn you first.'

'Thanks. I'm grateful.' The man might have some irritating habits but he *was* a loyal friend.

'Should you be keeping him waiting?'

Armitage shrugged. 'I told the messenger I had to get some more information from you before seeing Warren.'

Armitage had always been a bit too daring for his own good. His luck had begun to run out just before he got the job as Coroner's Officer. That had been the saving of him. The greater independence meant he had fewer senior policemen to answer to and to upset.

He winked. 'Luckily, the chiefs don't really know what this Coroner's Officer business is all about.'

Easy to fool them then. Sailing close to the wind again.

Best frowned then a thought occurred. 'There weren't any defensive wounds on his hands. Could it have been suicide?' he asked hopefully.

Armitage shook his head. 'He was left-handed.'

Best waited. More tamping and puffing. A little more Red Breast Flake. Best grabbed an imaginary knife in his left hand and made thrusts towards his own chest.

'It's possible. Not easy. But possible?'

'No,' said Armitage and took a long, satisfying draw. 'The wound was too far to the side. Wouldn't be able to get enough thrust behind it. In any case,' he added after a suitably significant pause, 'the knife went through his shirt. Suicides usually lift their clothes clear.'

Best nodded dispiritedly.

'All right,' he sighed, that hope gone.

'What about his property? Were there any items I missed?'

Armitage raised his eyebrows, 'I don't know what you saw but one item certainly is interesting. Very.'

He took another puff and shook his head enigmatically.

I'll kill him thought Best.

'Fortunately,' the pipe was out of the mouth now and jabbing in the direction of Best's chest, 'we hadn't got around to returning the property to his wife. Were going to of course when thought it was natural causes.'

'Good,' said Best and waited. Just *tell* me!

His old colleague reached into his briefcase, pulled out a cloth bag and tipped its contents over the desk top.

Spilling out were the objects he had seen briefly when he had looked through Myers' pockets last night in the dim light of the square: watch, coins, money clip, diary. SDF membership card.

'Clearly, if it was murder,' he said, 'robbery was not the motive.' That was a depressing thought. Robbery would have done nicely. Open and shut and no political repercussions.

Armitage nodded. 'Unless there was something else in his pockets which was no longer there when we found him.'

'Have to be worth a lot to someone to take it and leave this lot behind.'

He looked more closely at the silver pocket watch which seemed fairly new and quite impressive: one of those complicated affairs with several additional dials. One dial was for a chronometer the others showed seconds, days, dates and months.

'Why would he want a stopwatch? Was he an athlete?'

Armitage shook his head and shrugged. 'Don't know that much about him yet apart from the SDF stuff.'

Best inspected the watch chain's extra attachments: the vesta case and the miniature compass.

'And why a compass? Was he a walker?'

Perambulation was all the thing these days but somehow he couldn't see

Myers' taking trains to distant towns and walking back overnight just for the fun of it. 'Possibly been a surveyor, I suppose.' He shrugged, 'Or maybe he just wanted another fancy do-dah to festoon his watch chain.'

Best shook his head. 'Not that sort of bloke.' Even his own head was asking him how he came to that conclusion when he had not known the man.

'Might have been given him by his beloved. Women run out of ideas of what to give us once we have plenty of fancy shirt studs and cuff links.'

Sheepishly he took out his own watch chain upon which hung links holding a brass pencil, a seal and a vesta case in the shape of a skull.'

He pointed to the latter. 'She thought that very appropriate.' Obviously Armitage was not enamoured with the object. He had used a plain old matchbox for his pipe ritual.

One item he had seen but not examined was the gold tie pin the victim had been wearing. It was in the form of a wishbone holding a small ruby in it's cleft. Nothing noteworthy there.

But there was one other item which had rolled and fallen on the floor as the cache was emptied on the desk.

Armitage picked it up and, raising his eyebrows, placed it in Best's hands.

How did I miss that when I searched the body Best wondered?

'He had a second interior pocket on the left,' Armitage explained.

'A *secret* pocket?'

Armitage wrinkled his nose and inclined his head indicating perhaps but unlikely.

Inlaid around the bangle's sides were oval gold discs engraved with pictures of birds: a swallow, a bluebird, a robin and a dove. It looked like the sort of thing a younger woman might wear; pretty but neither staid nor substantial. Not a very precious item but not a cheap one either and its keeper chain was broken.

Best looked questioningly at Armitage. 'His daughter's - being taken to be mended?'

Armitage shook his head. 'He doesn't have a daughter – nor a granddaughter.'

The Coroner's Officer leaned forward suddenly and said, 'Oh, and there's *this*.'

He opened the diary, turned to day of Myers' murder and pointed at what was written there.

'Decide,' it said in large, loose letters underlined, 'whether to leave!'

Best stared at it. 'Leave what?' he muttered to himself.

'Exactly,' said Armitage, blew a long stream of smoke from the corner of his mouth and left for the Commissioner's office.

5

Best's presumption that this situation could prove volatile was quickly reinforced shortly afterwards by the news that the Commissioner wished to speak to him immediately. Also that Mr Henry Hyndman, leader of the Social and Democratic Federation, and prominent and pugnacious SDF member, Mr Jack Williams, were waiting downstairs to see him.

'Well, Best, what's this all about?' Commissioner Warren barked in his habitually abrupt manner. 'Tell me about last night. How you came across this man?'

Warren was an ex-military man appointed only a year earlier in the hope of bringing some discipline to the policing of public order.

Unusually, for a Commissioner, he did have some experience as a detective. In 1882 he had successfully investigated the disappearance in Egypt of a party of archaeologists and discovered that there were none of the suspected political ramifications. They had merely been ambushed and murdered by robbers.

Best refrained from informing Warren that two leading members of the Social and Democratic Federation were waiting downstairs to see him but concentrated on describing the events of the previous night in Trafalgar Square.

The Commissioner did not look at him as he spoke but allowed his gaze to wander up into the far corner of the room. He maintained this stance for several moments after Best had finished speaking then, at last, he lowered his eyes to announce, 'You, of course, will take over this enquiry.'

Best nodded, 'Yes, sir.'

It was a poisoned chalice but what could he do?

The head of his department would be furious about this direct communication with the Commissioner. To be caught between two ambitious and self-willed men was not a pleasant prospect.

Ex-Indian Civil Servant, James Monro, had hoped to lead the Metropolitan Police himself and felt that, as Assistant Commissioner Crime, he should have complete autonomy and answer only to the Home Office as had his predecessor, Howard Vincent. The previous Commissioner had become lazy and allowed this to take place but Warren would have none of it. He was the Commissioner and thus Commander-in-Chief.

'This case must be treated very discreetly. Nothing should be revealed to the Press until absolutely necessary. Until a charge is made, in fact.'

'But. . .' Best hesitated.

The Commissioner looked up in surprise. 'Yes?'

Best hesitated again then cleared his throat. 'Sir,' he said, 'we may not be *able* to *make* a charge without the help of the Press.'

Warren stared at him. Then said slowly and coldly, 'Help? From the Press?'

His reluctance was understandable. The press had not been kind to him. Unfortunately, fighting Kaffir wars, taking part in the second relief expedition to rescue General Gordon at Khartoum and putting down disturbances in Bechuanaland had not prepared him for a job in which tact, public relations and discreet handling of the press were major requirements.

It had not been an easy year for the new man what with the strain of policing the Jubilee celebrations, while keeping the Queen safe from Fenians bent to assassinate her. At the same time he had to deal with the furore following 'The Case of Miss Cass' in which a supposedly innocent woman had been arrested as a prostitute on Jubilee night.

True, the celebrations had gone well and the Queen was still alive but his handling of the Miss Cass case had been judged unfair towards the constable concerned. Neither had he impressed his current troops by later changing his mind about the constable's actions but failing to offer an apology.

No wonder police morale was low. Now there was all this political agitation and the annexing of Trafalgar Square. The new Commissioner had had a baptism of fire but his autocratic manner had forestalled sympathy and his adoption of a semi-military style uniform for everyday wear instead of occasional ceremonial wear had been seized upon with glee by the cartoonists.

The trouble with military men, Best had noticed, was they were not accustomed to the constant critical spotlight under which the police had to operate. Their battles took place in distant lands and comment on them was usually confined to whether they had won or lost ground to the native hordes and tended to favour the British military anyway. Mistakes could be hidden, glossed over or indeed metamorphose into triumphs. Not so in the police.

Best stood his ground.

'Yes, sir. I'm afraid we need the Press to help us find witnesses and get them to come forward. *Someone* must have seen *something* before we were called to the body.'

'But surely you enquired about this at the time?'

'Yes, but we had no idea then that it could be murder.' Good thing he doesn't know I was distracted by the search for Stark, Best thought. 'And people don't want their friends to see them helping us. But might come forward afterwards when they can do it discreetly.' Best cleared his throat again then added carefully, 'And in any case, don't you think that if we hold back too much now, when it *does* come out they will think we had some sinister motive? That there is more to all this than what we are saying?'

Warren stared at him.

A ranker was expressing an opinion and questioning his orders.

'The SDF are always trying to blame the police for everything,' Best blundered on and thought, why can't I just shut up? Oh, well, I could always become a publican. But he would hate that. Or he could go into the ice cream business like his uncle Antonio. But he would hate that too. What he loved was being a detective.

Warren continued to stare at him then sprang to his feet and began to pace, head down, behind his desk, his highly-polished boots gleaming and winking in the glow of the firelight.

Finally, he came to a halt, gave Best a direct glance from under his straight brows and thoughtfully stroked his heavy moustache.

'Right,' he said eventually. 'As soon as you are sure of the cause of death get Mr Williamson or Mr Monro to inform the Press. But,' he barked, 'Be discreet. Before that, keep it quiet.'

The old soldier was learning.

Best was painfully aware that the Press could already have been informed - by some hospital porter, ward maid or even a police officer.

The two gentlemen awaiting Best downstairs were an unlikely couple.

The weather-beaten, pugnacious, shaggy-bearded Jack Williams unapologetically declared his working class origins with his rough clothes and tweed cap.

The other man, Henry Mayers Hyndman, was also exactly what he appeared to be, a person of wealth and privilege.

At the age of forty-five Hyndman was firmly ensconced in self-important, corpulent middle age. His forehead was high and on the bulbous side, his beard flowing, and he was wearing his habitual garb of frock coat, impeccably tailored in Saville Row, and a black silk plush top hat from Lock & Co of St James's Street. His was unabashed upper-class attire which he maintained even when delivering speeches to the working classes and threadbare unemployed.

Could there be stranger bedfellows than these two? Hyndman was the well-to-do founder, leader and financer of the SDF; Williams, a proud member of the proletariat as well as an active member of the SDF Executive Council.

Best knew that many people wondered exactly what Hyndman was up to with his Social Democratic Federation particularly since he had once declared his opposition to universal suffrage. Was he merely trying to make a name for himself politically?

Best had heard both men speak on street corners and in Trafalgar Square and found them impressive in their different ways.

Williams, eyes alight with barely suppressed rage at the inequalities of the world gave fiery and challenging speeches bordering on the revolutionary.

Hyndman's bourgeois attire attracted attention from curious crowds who might not have paid the quite the same attention to a man in working class clothes.

He had lately become a declared devotee of Karl Marx, and now had the task, with his racy and argumentative speeches, of persuading his audiences that he had genuinely changed his earlier views. He admitted his privileged background but assured them, his restless blue eyes raking over them challengingly, that he now fervently believed in Universal Suffrage. Then this Eton and Cambridge educated gentleman would finish his speech by dryly thanking the audience for 'generously supporting my class'.

But Best knew from Special Branch colleagues that some socialists still didn't trust the man. Apparently his dictatorial manner was one of the reasons for the loss from their ranks of the likes of William Morris and Eleanor Marx who left to form the Socialist League.

Jack Williams did not appear to be a man without ego so why, Best wondered, had *he* stayed on?

The pair certainly now had a bond. At last year's Black Monday riot they both had been arrested and charged with conspiracy and sedition but had later been acquitted.

Best glanced from one to the other as they sat across the plain deal table in the sparse interview room. He expressed his condolences at their loss of one of their colleagues then said,

'Well, gentlemen. How can I help you?'

They looked at each other as though deciding who should speak first but

Hyndman clearly thought it was his prerogative and opened his mouth to do so. So did Williams.

Thus they spoke in unison to say,

'We know who is responsible.'

6

'Who?' asked Best scarcely daring to believe that the puzzle of Andrew Myers' death was about to be solved even before the definite cause had been established.

Hyndman was clearly not going to let his position as leader and spokesman be usurped again. He gave Williams a warning glance before announcing bluntly, 'Henry Champion.'

'But . . .' said Best, puzzled. If his memory served him right Henry Hyde Champion was another leading member of the SDF?

'I know what you're thinking,' Hyndman cut in.

Well, that's more than I do, thought Best.

'You're thinking how could this be? Champion is one of them.' He paused before saying dramatically, 'Well, he's not. Not any more.'

'Oh, I see,' said Best though he didn't really.

'He's resigned then?'

'No,' said Hyndman, 'he has been *expelled*.' The tone was triumphant.

This was a new motive for murder. He knew the Socialist Democratic Federation took their politics very seriously but ... There was a short silence before a frowning Best asked, 'And you think Mr Champion *killed* Andrew Myers?'

'That's putting it rather strongly,' corrected Hyndman sharply. 'But I'm convinced he was responsible, yes.'

Best was puzzled by these interpretations then remembered that the possibility that the man had been murdered had not yet been made public.

'Suppose you tell me how you came to your conclusions.'

'Very well, officer. He looked down at Best's hands. 'You might like to take notes.'

Best could see why people left his organisation. The man's manner was unbearably patronising. Some democrat. He suddenly became aware that Williams found all this somewhat embarrassing and had come along solely to try to keep a reign on his leader. He wasn't succeeding very well.

'I will hear your explanation first,' Best replied coolly, looking Hyndman right in the eye. 'If I deem it necessary, we will go through the story again and *then* I shall take notes.'

That was the way he liked to do it simply because the discrepancies between the first and the second telling could prove revealing.

He paused. 'First, may I ask why Mr Champion was expelled?'

'His ideas were not in accord with our aims,' Hyndman said bluntly.

'In what way?'

'I really can't see . . ' Hyndman huffed. There was a sore spot here.

'Humour me.'

'He declared himself to be a *Christian* Socialist,' Williams interposed, 'and didn't like the fact that Henry here is an atheist.'

Best waited, feeling that that was hardly an adequate reason for expulsion from a political organisation surely? There must be more.

'And he accused Henry of inciting violent revolution.'

Ah, he had *criticised* Hyndman.

Best nodded. 'And to go back to his 'responsibility' for the death of Mr Myers?'

'He was seen,' Hyndman hissed, 'last night, in the square.'

'Doing what?'

'Arguing with Mr Myers.'

'I see,' Best let the silence grow then said, 'and . . .?'

'The argument became very heated.'

Best waited.

'Almost came to blows, I hear.'

Ah.

'And he was with Mr Myers when he collapsed?'

'Yes!' Hyndman put in excitedly.

'We don't know,' said Williams.

Hyndman glared at him.

'And exactly whereabouts did this argument take place?'

'In the square,' Hyndman repeated firmly.

'*Whereabouts* in the square,' Best insisted.

'On the north side, on the upper pavement,' said Williams wearily.

'Ah, above the square. Not, exactly *in* it.'

'What difference!' exclaimed Hyndman.

'A great deal,' retorted Best.

'It was him who brought on Andrew's heart attack no matter what you say about whether he was here or there! You can't deny that.'

Wouldn't dream of it, thought Best breathing a sigh of relief but also of disappointment.

Hyndman was watching him, leaning forward then rocking back. He wants to say something but wonders whether he should, thought Best, which was quite surprising. Hyndman was a highly intelligent but clearly impetuous man. Suddenly it burst forth.

'He calls himself a *Christian* Socialist but do you know what he said after the workers broke the windows of some West End shops on Black Monday?'

Best shook his head. On Black Monday the SDF leaders had lost control of the mob who had run riot, smashing the windows of clubs of St James's (members of a club had derided them) and West End shops. The shaken SDF leaders had condemned their actions but pointed out that it was understandable.

'He said,' Hyndman exclaimed now, 'he said, "If I had a revolver and I saw a mob looting a shop I would shoot the fellows down right and left with my own hand!"'

Best sucked his teeth and shook his head endeavouring to appear duly shocked by this revelation. But you could not really blame Champion for reacting heatedly. The rampage had seriously harmed their cause.

Suddenly Hyndman said sadly, 'I shall miss old Myers,' and looked as if he meant it. 'He was an honest, decent man.'

So are you, in your fashion, thought Best, when your vanity doesn't get in the way.

There was another question begging to be asked although Best realised, given the previous conversation, what scorn would greet its utterance. He must find out to what the words written in the diary 'Decide whether to leave!' referred. Leave his marriage? His job? Or the SDF?

'You tell me that Mr Champion was no longer a member of the Social Democratic Federation and I know that several or your early members chose to leave to form the Socialist League . . .'

Hyndman looked at him sharply. 'Yes,' he said then adding briskly, 'A natural occurrence in the early days of any political movement.'

'Of course,' agreed Best then drew a deep breath. 'Had Mr Myers hinted that he wished to move on also?'

Hyndman glared at him open mouthed as if he had been slapped.

'Of course not! Haven't I just told you of the altercation between him and Mr Champion? Andrew was one of our staunchest members he would *never* have dreamed of leaving us.'

Best felt as if *he* had been slapped for not paying attention to what teacher was saying.

It was a curious sight. Crowds of onlookers peering over the wall into the sunken section of Trafalgar Square their eyes fixed on the people below.

Many of those on the pavement above had enjoyed a night at their clubs or the nearby theatres and restaurants. They had been drawn to rounding off their evenings by witnessing for themselves the amazing scenes they had been reading about in their daily newspapers: the occupation of this historical site at the heart of the capital by the rabble some of whom, they had been informed, had begun to carry the red banners of revolution on their marches.

The onlookers may well have been disappointed to see 'the rabble' forming orderly queues (women and children first) leading up to huge, steaming metal urns of hot tea and coffee.

It had been provided by the costermongers of Whitecross Market who had clubbed together to raise three pounds. With it they had bought sixty gallons of tea and coffee and several hundred portions of bread and cheese to hand out to the unemployed. Not surprisingly, the word had got around and the square was packed, which pleased Best greatly.

With luck this bumper crowd would contain some of his NFA witnesses. Witnesses with no fixed abode were a real headache for the police; so hard to track down. Who knows, Best thought optimistically, maybe even Stark will show his evil face for the sake of a hot cup of tea and some grub.

At least the onlookers would not be disappointed by the drama of the scene dramatically lit with flares held aloft by stalwart costermongers who were dressed to beat the increasingly frosty nights in overcoats, soft, tweedy caps and bowler hats.

Above and below. According to some commentators, this scene aptly and ironically illustrated what was wrong with the whole of British society: the well-fed and sanguine looking down on uncaringly on the hungry and desperate and sometimes throwing coins at them so they could see them scramble.

Best's companion in this NFA endeavour was, again, Constable Albert Roberts. A rather melancholy Constable Roberts.

'Florence has been berating me,' he revealed.

Ever since he had began studying the education pages of the *Police Guardian* Albert had been sprinkling his conversation with more formal words and berating was obviously one of his latest. His ultimate aims were to become a detective constable, pass his exams for sergeant, and marry Florence. Twelve hours duty a day was not helping him achieve any of these aims.

'What for?'

'Beating people.'

'Have you been?'

He shrugged. 'No, not me. I never went with that march.'

Three days earlier the Trafalgar Square crowd had set off on one of their intermittent marches, this time to the Mansion House in the City of London to see the Lord Mayor. The marchers had become unruly and now the S D F and the Socialist League were accusing the police of deliberately setting on the marchers, beating and kicking them and handing out similar punishment in the square the following day.

'They're calling us Warren's Wolves. I told her I never beat no-one,' said Albert momentarily forgetting his *Police Guardian* instructions about double negatives. He sighed and pulled at his chinstrap. 'She don't understand it gets frightening when the mob go mad. I try to tell her that we're only trying to keep order. That's our job.'

Best had to agree that it did seem rather hard, given that Florence had been glad of Albert's strong right arm when *she* had been under attack.

He, too, had been subject to some tart questions from his wife, Helen, about the alleged police brutality on the Lord Mayer's march.

And as they had left the interview room at Scotland Yard Hyndman and Williams hinted strongly that they really did not anticipate the police would be expending much energy chasing the man responsible for the death of their fellow member. They were clearly much too busy hounding the working class.

But what did they expect him to do about two men having a heated difference of opinion in the street? Even if, as they claimed, it had resulted in a heart attack for one of them? Of course *they* were not yet aware that he may have been murdered. He dreaded them finding that out.

'Have you told Florence that it can be frightening?' he asked.

Albert looked sheepish.

'Nah.'

Best could understand. The lad had won his lass by being protective, strong and unafraid.

'But it's different with a mob, innit? You don't know what they're going to do when they get inflamed, do you? Look at Chicago!'

A great many policemen were looking rather fearfully at Chicago, particularly those in Britain France, Germany and Ireland who were facing similar public unrest.

A bomb had exploded as police were clearing a crowd who had gathered in the Haymarket in Chicago last year. They had been agitating for shorter working hours and protesting about the police handling of a riot outside a factory during which a worker had been shot dead.

One police officer was killed instantly when the bomb exploded. Seven more died afterwards, as did several rioters.

Unsurprisingly, Albert had not been exactly delighted when he learned that he was to help track down the witnesses to the death of a member of the SDF, one of the two organisations he held responsible for his twelve hour days, abuse from the crowd, vermin infested uniform, separation from his beloved and now for turning her against him. This, apart from the threat of bombs: Fenian, Anarchist or socialist. All of them looked upon the police as enemies.

'We're always caught in the middle,' he complained.

Best knew he was waiting for advice on how to handle the Florence situation. He couldn't think of any except, 'Tell her that. That it's frightening.' He grinned. 'Make her a little fearful for you. That should do the trick.'

Albert grinned and nodded uncertainly. Best could understand how unappealing it might be for him to admit his frailty to a woman whom he had won with a strength honed at the section house boxing bouts.

He was saved from any more discussion on the subject by the sighting Joe Greton, the elderly man who had called them to the body last night. He went over to ask him to describe again how he had found it.

'He was just sitting here,' complained Greton, who stood, hot tea in one hand, ham roll in the other, in exactly the same place in which the dead man had been found the previous evening. 'He'd got my place and I wasn't 'aving that. I always sit here.'

He was repeating almost exactly what he said last night which could be a bad sign with some witnesses smacking as it did of a well-rehearsed, made-up story. But Best didn't think that applied in this case. Greton was merely hugging to himself a grievance deeply felt at the time which still rankled even though he knew the dead man could hardly have made way for him.

'Always sleeps upright for me chest and me arthritis,' he exclaimed revealing his few yellowing teeth sticking up like signposts between gaps and blackened stumps. Best was knocked back by the man's breath and rancid boy odour. 'If I lies down, I'd never get up again!'

Greton glanced longingly at his tea and ham roll. Best waited while he took a gulp, softened the roll in the hot liquid and took a soggy bite.

'Had he been there long?'

'Dunno.'

'How long between the time you saw him and when you called us?'

He paused while his tongue searched out stray bits of food from around his mouth; an unlovely sight.

'Couple of minutes. Wasn't going to let him take my place. Everyone knows that's my place.'

I'm sure they do, thought Best.

He turned to a younger witness, a little fellow who was hovering around behind Greton, eager to speak and claim his moment in the limelight.

His name turned out to be Hynchcliffe. When he got his audience with Best he stood straight up with arms by his sides stretching upwards to compensate for his lack of height. An ex-inmate from the Coram Street Foundling Hospital or some other orphanage Best wouldn't be surprised.

'He was there earlier, sir,' Hynchcliffe exclaimed fixing Best in the eye to ensure his attention. He was not totally successful in this as his left eye kept wandering a little to the right which was distracting. Best tried not to follow it with his gaze.

'How *much* earlier?' said Best concentrating on the good eye.

'Well, I ain't got no watch or nothing, course,' he sniggered at the thought. 'But, I would say, I saw him about half an hour earlier,' he hesitated, 'or so, I reckon.'

'What drew your attention to him?'

'He didn't look like one of us. He weren't posh or nothing but he *was* clean and had good boots.' In this world boots and their condition were a barometer of your current situation in life.

'An he looked sort of familiar an all.' He spread his hands. 'Course when I heard he was an SDF big bug it come to me I must have heard giving the spiel on the stump never realisin' I'd see him ready for the cold meat wagon.'

'Were his eyes open?'

'Nah.' Hynchcliffe rotated his head to relieve the stiffness in his neck caused by the stretching it up so high. Combined with the wandering eye the effect was disconcerting. 'If they had of been I expect I would have recognised him. But he was asleep. Like we found him later.'

'He was dead later.'

Hynchcliffe blushed. 'Yeh, well, but we *thought* he was kipping didn't we?'

'True.'

He was sorry to have embarrassed the lad. Orphanage inmates has this uncertain air about them and were easily crushed by those more used to the ways of the outside world.

'Earlier on, did you see anyone with him? Maybe someone who looked a bit different, like him?'

Hynchcliffe shook his head. 'Nah. Same people as there was later and they was all regulars.' He paused. 'Least I think so. No-one stuck out to me like he did.'

'And you saw no altercation in the vicinity?'

'No. Er, what?'

'Fight,' interrupted Albert, 'ruccus, barny, milling,' he went on throwing his *Police Guardian* lessons right out the window. 'Here,' he pointed downwards, 'right here on this spot.'

'Nah,' said Hynchcliffe. 'Would have been though if he'd been alive and refused to give old Joe his place.'

I believe that, thought Best.

7

'It's double-edged,' said PC Armitage the Coroner's Officer.

'I know,' said Best.

'I mean the weapon.'

'Oh. Then it was a dagger rather than a knife?'

'Which helps confirm it was murder.'

'I don't see why.'

Despite the news that the dagger wound had been the cause of death Best was still nursing the hope that Andrew Myers might have been in a sensitive frame of mind before the row with his old SDF comrade and that the unpleasantness had tipped him over. He had known suicide committed for less.

'He was a working man,' Best pointed out, 'so would probably have access to all kinds of knives – even double-edged ones.'

'And happened to have this one on him?'

'Why not? He could have come straight from work. Or maybe decided to kill himself and brought it with him. A dagger sounds dramatic, criminal even, but it's only a double-edged knife which could be used for all sorts of things.'

'Which can do more damage than a single-edged knife. Anyway,' Armitage said, planting the post mortem report on Best's desk, 'the other factors support the murder possibility.'

'I know, I know,' muttered Best before his old friend got the chance to stretch it out very slowly. 'No tentative test stabbings. No defence wounds on the hands. No letter in the pocket. The clothes not being lifted clear before the stabbing and all that. But there must be exceptions to all these rules.'

'Not that I've seen. And there's more,' he added triumphantly.

Thank goodness he hasn't taken his pipe out, Best thought. Has he run out of tobacco or what?

'Suicides usually crawl away somewhere private to die *or* do it dramatically where they can be seen by the maximum number of people.' He took a deep breath then jabbed his right forefinger at Best to emphasise his point. 'What *he* did was to die in a place as public as a Roman forum but no-one saw it happen. That doesn't make sense. *And,*' he added, 'another sign - *the weapon was not found . .* '

He sat back, content at having made his case.

Best shrugged dismissively. 'Not surprising given the venue. It could easily be lost or stolen – they take anything that can be sold on.'

But Armitage was still not finished. 'Most important of all, as I mentioned previously . . .'

'I know, I know. He was left-handed so it would have been difficult.'

'Difficult! Bloody impossible - particularly as it went in quite deep and severed . . .'

Best groaned.

'Why are you so determined to make it a suicide?' asked Armitage, genuinely puzzled. 'I admit it would be easier to tidy away, but it's not like you to be lazy.'

'I'm not, I'm not,' said Best plaintively, 'I just want to be certain what the evidence reveals. Even you, tucked away in your mortuaries and courts and running around on the Coroner's bidding must be aware how explosive this could be if it was murder?'

Best knew he was being unfair to his old friend who now retaliated.

'Bury your head in the sand if you want. Is that what happens when you become a famous Scotland Yard detective. You think you can be godlike and alter reality just for the sake of appearances! Well good luck!'

Henry Hyde Champion was another wealthy male endeavouring to relieve the poor of their suffering and free them from their shackles. Best had learned this much from Williams and Hyndman although they had not put it in these precise terms.

They had explained that Champion was the son of Major General Champion. As an officer in the Royal Artillery "H H", as his friends called him, he had served with some distinction in the Second Afghan War but had returned to England suffering from typhoid.

They had also explained that Mr Champion was inclined to act too much on his own initiative to be an effective member of a democratic organisation such as theirs.

Best saw a handsome, slightly built, aesthetic-looking man of about thirty years of age. He had the inevitable self-confidence of the privileged male but his direct gaze was earnest and sincere.

The eyes were fine, the nose straight, the chin clean-shaven and the moustache quite modest but his hair was parted in the middle and held close to the head in fashionable romantic-poet style. Not without vanity then.

After politely enquiring about his health and likelihood of a return to his duties as a Royal Artillery officer Best learned that even before Champion's illness brought him back to Britain he had become disenchanted with his military role.

Indeed, at Kabul, this Royal Artillery officer found he was not suitably delighted by the capture of seventy-five abandoned enemy field guns nor the massacre of three thousand tribesmen against a loss of only ninety-six British soldiers.

'We had no business *being* there,' he exclaimed then leaned forward and confided earnestly, 'When I realised I was expected to take part in the Egyptian and Sudanese campaign merely to protect our financial and strategic interests, I resigned.' There was a look of distaste on his face.

It seemed his conscience had been awakened in other ways since and he was keen to explain how. Like wealthy socialist Hyndman, he too would have come up against scepticism about his motives.

'My recuperation allowed me much opportunity to read,' he explained 'specifically the works of Marx, Engels and John Stuart Mills.' He paused. 'Then I looked about me and saw what they were talking about.'

Hyndman had conceded that Champion had been a keen and financially-generous a supporter of the SDF and had edited their journal, *Justice*. The reasons for the parting must have been strong and feelings aroused even more so.

'But you were expelled from the Social Democratic Federation,' Best said abruptly.

Champion nodded and smiled. 'Yes. I have joined the Fabian Society.'

Forthright in other areas he was clearly keen to brush over the SDF split in gentlemanly fashion, which was more than Hyndman had been.

'I understand you may have been the last person to speak to Myers that night?'

Champion looked startled. 'Was I?' He paused. 'Who told you that?'

'Mr Hyndman and Mr Williams.'

A slow smile spread over Champion's handsome face. 'Do they now? And how would they know that?'

'Another member saw you. Isn't it true?'

'Oh, yes. Well, I certainly spoke to him. We bumped into each other on the pavement above the square.'

Best waited.

Champion looked regretful. 'How sad that my last words with an old comrade should have been such angry ones.' He studied his impeccably manicured hands. 'How very sad.' He looked directly at Best. 'I've heard that there is some suggestion that the poor man was murdered? Is that correct?'

'Yes.'

He looked shocked.

'Why would anyone want to do *that*?'

'That's what we are trying to find out.'

There was a short silence which Best broke by saying, 'Tell me about him. What was Andrew Myers like?'

Champion was momentarily disconcerted by this change of tack. He'd clearly expected to be asked what the argument had been about. Which was exactly why Best had not done so. Abruptly changing tack was a useful ploy, particularly when interviewing confident, educated people. Anything to shake that implacable confidence just a little.

In fact, he was eager to know the answer. It would help bring the murder victim to life, to get a feel of his personality and why someone would want to kill him. Grieving, distraught relatives were of little use in this respect even if they knew how outsiders viewed the victim. A word picture from a colleague or friend, particularly one who was a journalist, could be invaluable.

'Oh, well,' Champion said, steepling his hands and bringing the tips of his fingers up to his lower lip. 'He was a nice chap. Honest. Firm in his opinions.'

Ah. Argumentative.

'A docker by trade. Very keen on the Federation.'

'Did he make enemies. You know, with these firm opinions of his?'

A slight smile tugged at Champion's lips then came an expansive spread of hands. 'Oh, well Inspector, we all make enemies when we take up the banner, don't we?'

Ah. He wasn't going to say. Not yet, anyway.

'But I understand you were having a violent argument?'

Champion sat back, 'Oh heavens, no. I wouldn't say that. A strong disagreement, perhaps.'

'About what?'

'Religion.'

Oh, that which supposed to make brothers out of men but so often drove them apart, even so far as to make them want to kill each other.

'Amongst other things.' He sighed. 'To be honest, and I hesitate to say this now he is dead and unable to defend himself, it wasn't really a disagreement. I was attacked - verbally, that is - and was merely defending myself. I don't think I even raised my voice – no matter what Mr Hyndman and Mr Williams claim.'

To be honest, Best could not imagine Henry H Champion raising his voice. But, as he knew from experience, you could never really tell about people and recalled Hyndman saying that Champion would shoot looters out of hand. Obviously, the man was not quite as mild as he appeared.

'Now, just let me ask you to help me pinpoint his movements and the timing. Can you remember what time you met?'

Champion beetled his brows in an effort to recall the moment.

'Well, I'd been to my club and left about eleven fifteen I think it was and I decided to stroll down to the square to see what was happening. So, I think it would be about 11.30pm.'

'What did you expect to be happening?'

He shrugged. 'One can never tell.'

'How long did you and Myers talk?'

'Well, as I said, I couldn't say we talked at all. I was harangued, more like.'

Best was puzzled. 'About religion?'

He held his hands in prayer form and softly tapped them together as he tried to find the right words. 'What it was, was that he was still angry about my criticism of Hyndman's atheism. Not that I had actually criticised *that*, it was mainly that I felt it encouraged him to be more cavalier in his incitement of the unemployed – not considering the consequences sufficiently.'

Asking whether he thought Myers was thinking about leaving the Federation seemed even more pointless than asking Hyndman. If Myers had been so vigorously defending the Federation's founder it was hardly likely he was about to leave. Unless, of course, Champions criticisms had sown doubt in his mind and he had really been arguing with his own conscience.

'Had he been drinking, do you think?' Best asked instead.

Champion frowned. 'Well, if he had I didn't notice the signs. It was more as if this was something he had wanted to get off his chest for some time and the opportunity suddenly arose and he let fly. Of course, he added thoughtfully, 'a drink or two may have fuelled his ire.'

'So, I presume you were walking eastwards from St James's and he westwards?'

Champion nodded. 'Yes.'

'And when you parted, he continued westwards?'

'Yes.'

'Did he say where he had been?'

'No. Down in the square, I presumed.'

'Had you seen him talking to anyone else?'

'No. I hadn't seen him at all until we were suddenly face to face.'

'Who else was in the square at the time? I mean among your political friends and acquaintants?'

'I didn't see anyone else.'

'Well, I think that's all for the moment. Thank you.'

Best began to stand up to take his leave.

'Anything I can do, just let me know.'

'I will, thank you. Oh,' Best held his right forefinger in the air as though a thought had just struck him, 'was Mr Myers instrumental in your being expelled from the Social Democratic Federation?'

'Oh, yes. Very.'

8

There was no mistaking that this was a dock area, Best thought as he strode down East Smithfield in the misty, chilly dawn light.

Nautically-named pubs straddled the corners: The Jolly Tar, The Trade Winds, The Anchor. Ships chandlers abounded offering all that might be needed on voyage from shiny brass quadrants and chronometers to cases of meat and biscuits guaranteed to survive any climate. There were even hammocks strung up outside and swaying in the wind.

The tar, himself, was also adequately catered for with tough canvas trousers, warm dreadnought jackets and waterproof nor' westers with which to brave Atlantic storms.

But it wasn't all salt-water practicalities. There was a surprising surfeit of frivolous items in establishments specialising in gifts for wives, girlfriends and mothers: gaudy scarves, handkerchiefs and parasols, and jewellery with more sparkle than substance. Best knew that, once bought, some of these "presents" would be sold back to the shops by the local prostitutes who acquired them from drunken sailors.

Should all this evidence of things maritime escape the unobservant they would soon be alerted by the endless rattle and trundle of the passing cabs and wagons laden with people and cargo and pavements alive with pig-tailed Chinamen; mulatto Chilenos; Spaniards with bright handkerchiefs about their heads and black, woolly-haired Colombians.

Looking rather out of place among all this exoticism would be dark suited, earnest-looking missionaries carrying Bibles and tracts in many languages.

More in evidence at this early hour, however, was the tramping army of workmen advancing on the docks in increasing numbers. Not only were they also drab in comparison with colourful foreign sailors but many were paler, thinner and more poorly dressed: elbows out of thin, greasy jackets which were buttoned up to the throat to keep out the early morning chill; boots only just holding together at the seams.

Their expressions as they trooped their way to the dock gates were a mixture of resignation, hope and grim determination. As their numbers grew, they began to jostle each other, constantly trying to get ahead, grunting as they did so, as if gaining an advantage at this stage might make a crucial difference later.

Best took out his warrant card ready to show to the bored policeman on the dock gate whose principal duty was the hopeless task of preventing theft from the ships cargoes.

The card was almost knocked out of his hand as the pace of the crowd quickened into a run. All were going in the same direction heading for the same point - the dockyard railings. On the other side of the railing stood two tall, wooden structures which to Best looked like a cross between church pulpits and a bathing huts.

He realised the reason for the sudden rush. Climbing the stairs up to one of these pulpits was a middle-aged man wearing a straw hat and carrying a register. The caller-on or calling foreman was about to start work. Several more of his ilk were taking their places behind the dockyard railings. The cage it was called.

As the first caller-on began reading names out from his book eager hands shot up accompanied by calls of 'Here! Here!'

Some of those not called tried to scramble onto the backs of others so they could be seen, shouting out the caller-on's name, or their own names to remind him who they are and that they were there, grinning to encourage him to select them. Cockney voices. Irish voices. The heavily accented guttural voices of Poles, Germans and Russians. Cutting sharply through this foreign babble was the occasional posh, very English voice of someone who had seen much, much better days.

The jostling became desperate, manic even. Men began scuffling, shouting and scrambling as they thrust their hands into the air trying to catch the attention of a man who might grant them a day – or even half a day's work. Sometimes less.

The attitudes of the callers-on varied wildly. Some appeared blithely indifferent to the wild scene before them. Others just got on with choosing their favoured men then let the rest scramble for their remaining passes. The eyes of one nervously watched the hands of the men who reached towards him through the railings. His face showed signs of recent contact with a fist.

All this for work not in the least pleasant, thought Best. Harsh and backbreaking work, sometimes even literally, which earned only the pittance of five pence an hour.

Those few chosen, the younger, bigger, stronger men, stepped forward gratefully to collect their precious labour tickets. The many not selected turned away slowly, hesitantly, trying to decide whether it was worth staying around in the hope that a favourable wind might blow in more ships. But fewer ships relied entirely on sail now.

Tomorrow, Best knew, these casuals would go through the same thing again while they and their families became more and more hungry and they themselves less fit for work. Some sat down and cried.

It was a heart-rending and demeaning scene. Small wonder we are on the edge of a revolution, thought Best. No surprise that after last year's riot Jack Williams had led a raggedy band of unemployed whistling the Marseillaise into a church with a well-to-do congregation or that red flags were taking the place of the black banners of desperation usually carried by unemployed marchers.

He took a deep breath and entered the dockyard, trying to shake off the effects of these sad sights so as to concentrate his mind on the serious matter in hand.

He picked his way among the hundreds of barrels of sherry piled up between the cliff-like warehouses stacked with wool, tea and spices; the strangely mixed smells greeted him before he ever set eyes on the goods. To his right were the wooden transit sheds fronted by hydraulic cranes for lifting heavy goods from the ships. He made his way through an alley to the busy North Quay.

At the North quay a steamer flying the Spanish flag had already begun unloading oranges, lead and cork. Alongside, a splendid clipper, its sails neatly furled, had brought in tallow, wool, animal hides and lead-coloured copper ore, the stench of the hides at odds with the beauty of the vessel.

As the docks swung into action the noise level grew: coopers hammering casks and rolling them thunderously along the wharf; cranes creaking and rattling as their heavy chains loosed their loads; wagon wheels crunching over cobbles; ropes splashing into the water and orders and curses shouted in many languages. There was even the occasional song as crew members still on board prepared their breakfast, the familiar smell of their frying bacon mingling with cargo smells.

Over at the West Quay a row of outward bound vessels were loading up with crates of British manufactured goods. Judging by how far they had dropped below the level of the quayside some were almost fully loaded. The stevedores, who had been working all night, were obliged to climb down into the boats while precariously balancing their heavy loads. Small wonder so many dockers were maimed or killed.

It was at the Eastern Dock that Best found who he was looking for. The man reputed to know everything there was to know about the London Dock, dockmaster, Bernard Mulcahy. He turned out to be a big man in every sense with crinkly fair hair and small blue eyes in a craggy, red face. His expression, when Best introduced himself, was guarded.

Mulcahy was a member of one of the powerful London Irish clans of stevedores. Regular men, permanent men who never needed to scrabble by the dock gates. Stevedores loaded the ships, considered much more skilled work than unloading them.

Best nodded in the direction of the gates and said, 'It's a bit desperate down there, isn't it?'

Starting off with a casual comment could be the best way of dealing with an unwilling witness and Best sensed that Mulcahy was unwilling.

Mulcahy shrugged. 'Worse down at the Albert and the East India.'

'Why's that?' asked Best even though he knew the answer.

The Albert and East India were further from the centre of London and it as them which suffered first when things got hard like they were now.

'Customers don't want to cart their goods a few extra few miles.' He shrugged. 'And now Tilbury is doing the dirty on us cutting their fees.'

Tilbury was much much further away, near the mouth of the Thames, so had struggled during its first years but since it had reduced its docking fees it was winning business away from the docks up river.

They had reacted by reducing the dockers' wages even further and cutting down on the number of permanent men. This in turn widened the pool of casuals whom they could hire and fire at will. It was an every increasing downward spiral.

'I expect some of them enjoy the power,' Best said inclining his head towards a caller-on who was passing by with his 'bible' of preferred names tucked under his arm.

'Oh, aye. Some do. Some do.'

'I noticed one of them had a black eye.'

Mulcahy relaxed a little and laughed. 'An occupational risk.'

'They get threatened?'

'Some do. Some do.' He paused then muttered. 'Some deserve it.' He paused again, looked directly and Best and said. 'I heard about old Andrew Myers. What's that all about?'

'I don't know. I was hoping you might tell me?'

He looked startled. The guarded look returned and Best cursed himself.

'I mean, tell me what sort of bloke he was? And what work he did here?' he put in quickly. 'I just need to get a picture of him.' God, I sound more like old Chief Inspector Cheadle every day he thought. Him and his pictures.

'Well,' Mulcahy hitched up his trousers as he gave the matter some thought. 'He did a lot of things,' he said carefully. 'Different jobs. Started out doing a bit of mechanics – keeping the cranes running and that stuff. But that didn't fill up his time so he did a bit of gate duty, then helped out in the office – accounts and suchlike.'

So, he hadn't exactly been a docker in the manner Best had imagined. 'Nothing really physical then?'

'No. No. Not so's you'd notice,' Mulcahy murmured dryly. Best let that past but noted it.

'And was he liked?'

'Yeh, I suppose so. Nothing you could take exception to, you know. An average sort of bloke really. But he had got a bit up there.' He tapped his forehead. 'Can't deny that I suppose. But just an average bloke really.'

Best let a silence grow. There was clearly more there. But would it come out? Silence was his best ally. Many people were unnerved by silences and rushed to fill them.

'I must say,' Mulcahy said at length, 'I was surprised when *he* became a big bug with the SDF. Being an average sort of bloke an all.'

Best nodded. Jealousy there? Or had he been rocking the boat by recruiting for the SDF? The stevedore clans might not like that. Changes could ruin their monopoly.

The man clearly was burning to say more so he applied the pressure by starting to turn away and saying, 'Well, thank you very much. If there is anything else you can think of . . .?'

Mulcahy's lips tightened involuntarily as if at some private thought and he shook his head slowly. A slight smile began to twitch at the corners of the big Irishman's mouth.

'What?' said Best briskly.

'Oh, nothing.'

'Come on! The man's dead. You must want to help find out who killed an old colleague.'

Mulcahy shrugged. 'Well, it was just a rumour.' He shook his head. 'Only a rumour.'

'So it won't matter if you tell me what it was, will it?' Best said casually. He smiled patiently.

Mulcahy grimaced and inclined his head in partial agreement. 'I suppose.' He couldn't resist now.

'Rumour had it that Myers had had a heavy threat.'

'A death threat?'

He nodded.

'Who from?'

'A bunch of the casuals.'

'Why would they do that?'

'Because he wouldn't give them work, of course. They reckoned he had it in for them because they were Poles.'

Best was stunned. 'Are you telling me now that he was also a caller-on?'

Mulcahy nodded. Quite pleased with himself. 'Oh, yeh, that was his last job here. He was a caller-on – a contract man.'

9

Florence was the first to arrive that morning at the Salvation Army Rescue Offices in Hackney. She hung up her army bonnet on the peg board by the wall, tidied her hair, settled down at the Enquiry and Help department desk and began the final read through of *The War Cry*'s 'Missing' column.

The column was due at the printers that morning and she knew from experience that it was very important to make sure that all the names and details were correct. She had learned to her cost, how easily mistakes could slip through. Somehow, a letter 'a' could stray away from its place or a rogue 'b' insert itself where it was not wanted. Even a whole word could become misplaced almost as though it had a will of its own and had gone off looking to make mischief. Once the page was printed these mistakes would leap out at you, gleefully waving.

At least that was how Florence saw it although she knew she must keep this whimsical view to herself. Mrs Bramwell Booth, the General's daughter-in-law, would not approve and the Missing column was one of that lady's responsibilities.

Instead of appreciating how easily such errors could be made there seemed to be a general feeling that they were the result of nothing other than carelessness, sheer carelessness and carelessness was something deplored.

Florence could recite the column's introduction by heart which was not a good thing. Over-familiarity made the words more susceptible to error – you saw what you expected to see - so she concentrated that much harder.

In the introduction, Mrs Booth offered to assist in finding 'missing friends, lost daughters and prodigal sons' in this or other countries. She assured all correspondents of strict confidentiality and instructed that letters should be written (in any language) and addressed to: Enquiry, 259, Mare Street, Hackney, London, N. E.

In fact, this was the first time that Florence had seen this particular

'Missing' list. Yesterday she had been out with a cadet teaching her how to sell *The War Cry*. So she now scanned it both with interest and minus the handicap of undue familiarity.

First, came Jessie Loving, who had been placed in an orphanage and destitute home by her parents some years before and had lost touch with them when the children from this orphanage had been sent abroad. Now Jessie had returned to England and was desperate to be re-united with her parents, Mrs and Mrs Loving. Could this really be their name? If so, how poignant. Florence checked back through the actual letters and finally decided that Loving was the only possible interpretation of a name written in the painfully school-girlish but clear hand.

Then there was 'a case of cruel desertion'. A Mrs Bradbury sought her husband Herbert who had left her 'helpless and penniless with a child to support'.

The missing Herbert was thirty years old, 5ft 5inches in height, very dark, with a cast in his left eye, a lump on his left cheek and spoke Italian and French.

The enclosed photograph ('to be included whenever possible') confirmed what Mrs Bradbury probably already knew, that Herbert had been no great catch in the first place. Florence grinned at the naughtiness of this thought while at the same time chastising herself for its ungodliness. All men couldn't be handsome, kind and strong like Albert.

She shouldn't have accused him of being one of Warren's wolves. He wasn't like that. Hadn't he saved her – her prince. They had teased each other about their names: one after a Prince and the other after a heroine with a lamp and decided that, between them, they should be able to keep the world safe.

Back at the missing list two sets of distressed parents were seeking their sons, one of whom had left home to become a street firewood seller in Birmingham and failed to write home since. All these pleas were sad but run of the mill.

Ah, but here was something interesting - the strange case of Florence Rilkestone, a milliner's apprentice. This particular Florence had been sent to Barnsbury in North London by her employer three months ago to pay Queen's taxes to the tune of £3.2s.0d. and had not been heard of since. The taxes remained unpaid.

Florence Rilkestone was fair, slight and ladylike and 'not yet fourteen'. But here was a clue. (Florence could not resist becoming caught up in some of 'the cases'.)

'Florence frequently attended the Holloway I. Barracks.'

The 'I', she presumed, stood for infantry. What a strange way of putting it, 'frequently attended'. Did it mean she hung around the gates? She worked there? Or what? She checked that the odd name, 'Rilkestone' was correct and managed to resist reading the rest of the letter. Perhaps later, if she had time.

Suddenly she was drawn into a more dramatic case headed:

"**EVERYBODY'S BUSINESS**: - *Read this, and then help to find* **MISS VIOLET JANE JEFFRIES**."

It transpired that about ten months ago Miss Jeffries had taken a train from Manningtree in Essex bound for Liverpool Street Station in London.

"*The facts of the case are very distressing,*" the item continued, "*and can only be fully known by the young lady being brought to light.*"

How curious. Pregnant and deserted most likely. Maybe by her own father – Florence had learned how common this was - and her very life feared for. The distance was short from Liverpool Street to the murky Thames with its dark and unforgiving currents.

She must read that letter as well, when she had a moment.

But it was the final case in the missing list which caused Florence stop and catch her breath.

"**DECOYED OR STRAYED**:- *On Friday last, a little girl of 10 or 11 years, named PHILLCOCKS, disappeared from 14 Peabody Buildings, Commercial Street, Whitechapel. Her parents are heartbroken at her prolonged absence, and fear the worst that could happen to her. Appearance: dark blue eyes with a slight cross, brown hair, rather thin face, mark on thigh, height, 3ft 9 inches.*"

Florence covered her eyes. Oh, please God, no, she pleaded to herself before giving in to the insistent calls from her newly arrived colleagues that she join their circle welcoming in the new day by singing together:

Around me in the world I see
No joy that charms me out of Thee,
*   Its honours fade and fall;*
But with Thee, though I mount the cross,
I count it gain to suffer loss,
*   For Thou art All-in-all!*

'The difficulty is,' said Best to Albert, 'how we can find out *which* gang had it in for Myers.

Albert nodded sympathetically. He loved to share his troubles with others but was always endearingly interested in theirs as well. As far as he was concerned all inner life must be revealed. There was no point in not doing so.

He had extracted the latest information on Myers from the tired Detective Inspector who, in any case, felt Albert deserved to be brought up to date because he had been in at the beginning.

With his natural curiosity about people, Best thought, Albert might make a good detective. Of course he would have to pass his educational exams first and learn to curb his inclination to share his problems. Imagine the mayhem that could cause when handling a delicate case? Being able to keep your own counsel was a vital trait for a successful detective.

'What you need is somebody to go into the dock as a casual labourer,' Albert said.

'I know. But there is nobody to spare. Sergeant Smith has got a big case of his own and what with this' he stretched out his right hand to encompass the square and all its problems, the Jubilee, the Fenians . . .'

'I'll do it,' Albert said suddenly. 'If they'll let me.'

Best looked him up and down. 'You're much too clean and healthy looking.'

'I can transform myself,' he said using one of his new words. 'Dirty up. My dad has some old boots and a cap he wears down at the allotment. An' I can put a bit of flour on my face to make it pasty.'

'You look strong.'

'Well, that's all right innit? It means I might get called on.'

'But these gangs are mostly foreign and you haven't any languages.'

He looked a bit crestfallen at that but thought a bit then shrugged. 'I've picked up a few words here and there. Was born in Bethnal Green, don't forget. Anyways, the other casuals are bound to gas about it, ain't they?' He looked about him. 'Be more interesting than standin' 'ere all day, wouldn't it?'

He was right there.

'You want to be closer to Florence.'

'Well, it would make me feel easier,' he admitted. 'Could keep a look out for Stark as well.'

He knows exactly what to say to persuade me, thought Best.

'It might be dangerous. Florence wouldn't thank me for getting *you* killed.'

Albert drew himself up, 'I can look after myself.'

Indeed, Albert was the undefeated champion of his section house boxing club.

'They don't play by the Queensbury Rules down there you know,' Best warned. 'And your sneaky left hook won't help much if you're set upon by a gang, will it? Don't forget you won't have the protection of your uniform.'

Oddly enough that came as a jolt of surprise to some officers when they first became detectives.

Best was torn. No doubt Albert was a big man and had a reputation for being able to look after himself. Then again Warren was anxious to get this murder solved and he'd be well pleased if it could be proved that the murder was the result of a workplace feud or resentment rather than being dangerously political.

'I'll have a word.'

A filthy small boy with wild, tawny hair was tugging at Albert's sleeve and shouting, 'Here, mister! Here, mister!'

Albert's friendly face encouraged both adults and children to approach him without fear.

'Found this,' said the lad. He held up a knife, or more precisely a dagger, almost piercing Albert's hand with it.

From what Best could see peeping between the boy's grimy fingers it was no ordinary dagger. Not very large, about nine inches from end to end, with a dark wooden handle mounted with brass and silver. What was most unusual about it was the shape of the etched silver blade.

The lower edge curved inwards from the handle end then belled out before turning upwards, culminating in a fine point. It reminded Best of nothing so much as Ali Baba's slippers in a nursery story.

The second most surprising thing about this dagger was its weight. When Albert placed it in his hand Best almost dropped the weapon. The delicacy of the blade had led him to expect a much lighter object.

Only one edge was sharpened, he noticed, but the unsharpened side was thin and fine enough to act as another cutting edge when plunged into a body.

Clinging around the tip and edges of the blade were dark, gritty marks, which might be blood. More were embedded in the etching in the centre.

Best held it at the ends so the gritty stains would not rub off before it could be deduced whether they were in fact blood. Unfortunately, there was no way of finding out whether the blood was animal or human.

He examined the etching under a street lights. It turned out to be a type of highly-ornamental script somewhat similar to Arabic but intertwined with scrolls and whirls. Neither Best nor Albert could make anything of it.

'It looks more like a ceremonial object to me than a serious weapon,' said Best.

'Bit small for that innit?' asked Albert. 'Don't they use bloody great swords for ceremonies?'

'For *our* ceremonies,' Best agree. 'But those of other races could use something like this. It's very ornamental.'

'Yeh, I suppose. An' it *is* foreign, innit.'

'*Yes. Isn't* it,' emphasised Best. Albert insisted that Best correct his English but it made him feel a bit too like a schoolmaster so he tried to do it by example. 'It looks Eastern.'

The urchin was hovering impatiently, stretching up his head to remain in their sightline, his eyes shifting from one man to the other expectantly.

'Good lad,' said Albert patting him on the head, risking another lice invasion.

'Yes,' said Best and reached into his pocket for some coins.

Both knew that the boy's father, if he had one, would probably box his ears if he knew his son had brought them an object that might be worth a few pounds.

'Where did you find this, son?' Best asked as he placed the coins in the grimy paw.

The boy swivelled round and pointed towards one of the now dry fountains. 'Over there.'

'Show us.'

He nodded, straightening up. He was important now. He marched over to indicate the spot, tucked just below the fountain rim.

The attire that Albert chose for his first day out in plain clothes could scarcely be described as that of a typical dock casual. But then there really was no such thing.

Most of these unemployed men had done other kinds of work. They were old soldiers and sailors, out-of-work Government clerks, bankrupt master butchers and bakers, servants who had lost their characters - sometimes due to dishonesty - sometimes to unjust accusations of dishonesty, farm labourers driven into the city by the desperate situation in the countryside and permanent dock labourers thrown out of work so now having to scramble for it with the rest of the unemployed.

There were even pickpockets with hands so shaky from drink that they could no longer perform successfully and burglars who had lost the knack or whose appearance had deteriorated so much that they could not go unchallenged in the better neighbourhoods.

Thus, the clothing of the casual dock labourer could be described as varied. Most often it was threadbare but often with a dash of bravado or some hint that the wearer had once been respectable.

Albert had given a lot of thought to his disguise. The chief items of clothing he chose were an old pair of dark blue fustian trousers frayed around the bottoms and a little out at the knee and a threadbare tweed jacket and matching waistcoat, all purchased at a nearby slop shop out of his plain clothes allowance.

Dad's old gardening boots proved ideal: worn down, scuffed, cracked across the top and ingrained with soil. Oddly, they also proved more comfortable than the ones supplied by the Metropolitan Police. Warren, to his credit, had complained about the poor quality of constable's boots - as well as that of the police horse's saddles – and he was right.

He chose a collarless shirt and around his throat tied a dark red and brown neckerchief which he kept touching anxiously feeling strangely vulnerable without his high-buttoned police tunic.

But the *piece de resistance* was the cap. (Not that he knew such an expression yet but French lessons were on his agenda once he had learned to use his own language properly. He was only too aware how great a help that a second language was in becoming a Scotland Yard detective.)

The cap was also his father's having been part of his uniform as a driver on one of the Great Eastern Railway horse-vans which fanned out all over London from their stables in Bethnal Green.

The pill box shape was still quite stiff and smart and the GER badge remained in place but the cap had been taken out of service as being unsuitable for someone representing one of the great railway companies due to a deep crack right down the middle of its shiny peak.

Albert wore it at a rakish angle and reckoned this jauntiness, the feeling the cap had seen better days plus the indication of an earlier occupation was just right.

To complete the picture his clean and healthy young skin had been suitably sullied with a two-day beard growth and an application of flour mixed with coal dust.

It pleased him that none of the battalion of unemployed marching towards the dock gates gave him a second glance. But of course they never looked at each other very much anyway. They were concentrating on how they could ensure that *this* was the day they got work.

The real test would come when he faced the caller-on.

10

There was no doubt about it, the victim's widow, was a surprise. There was a hypnotic aura about this handsome and slightly severe-looking woman who had olive skin, lustrous, deep-set dark eyes and blue-black hair worn around her head in a thick plait. Best felt as if something volatile within her was being held back. But she could just be struggling to restrain her grief.

Mrs Adeline Myers was also, Best imagined, a cut above her husband socially. But then, how much did he really know about the man? He must learn more, quickly.

It may have been only two days since her husband's death but Mrs Myers was already a symphony in good quality, fashionable, black. The bodice of her dress (crape of course) was snugly-fitting and the front of the skirt was draped in shepherdess style while, at the back, the gathered drapes fell into graceful folds. Very becoming.

Heavy jet jewellery had once served the purpose of alleviating the obligatory dull mat of the gown but it was fast going out of mourning fashion. In its place Mr Myers had tied a black moiré bow at her neck and tiny blue black steel beads were scattered over her net cap. The shot moiré glowed and the beads glinted subtly as she moved. Neither item breeched mourning etiquette rules with vulgar, tasteless shine.

Clearly the services of either Jays or Peter Robinson's mourning warehouses had been swiftly sought. Even the delicate handkerchief she held was edged with black.

Best's knowledge of these mourning matters had been derived from his friend and colleague, John George Smith, whose mother had taken in laundry for the gentry, and also his wife Helen who found all the rules highly amusing.

Perhaps I'm being unfair, he thought. She may have already been in mourning for another loved one. One never knew. But it would have to have been a *recent* bereavement since fashionable ladies did not countenance old-fashioned mourning wear and, Adeline Myers appeared to be quite a fashionable lady.

Nonetheless, he was relieved and grateful that he did not have to cope with a sobbing or hysterical woman.

'He was a good husband,' she said simply, spreading her hands expressively.

That seemed a rather strange thing to say at this stage but, as Best knew, people reacted differently to sudden death. What he would really like to know is was her husband thinking of leaving her? But this was hardly the moment to ask.

'It must have been a great shock to you,' he said. 'My condolences.' And he meant it having suffered dreadful loss himself more than once.

'I still can't believe it.' Her voice had an unusual lilt and her words were carefully enunciated as with some foreigners but he could detect no trace of foreign accent.

She looked up as her parlour maid wheeled in the tea trolley. 'I'll leave it to you on this occasion, Maud,' she said and the girl gave a little bob and nodded gingerly. Interesting. Mrs Myers was obviously a stickler for the proprieties. He wondered whether she had seen the primitive scrambling for work at the dock gates presided over by her husband. Nothing very proper about that.

The Myers' residence, a substantial red-brick villa in Hackney, had also been something of a surprise. The level, not perhaps of great wealth but certainly of comfort, spoke of means greater than those available to a mere caller-on or contract man. He must delve deeper into the money aspect. But not now.

'I'm sorry to ask you such a question at a time like this,' Best said as he accepted the delicate porcelain cup and saucer proffered by Maud, 'but can you think of anyone who might want to do your husband any harm?'

He spoke calmly and carefully. He had accepted the offer of refreshment so as to keep the interview on an informal footing and to distract the grieving widow. In his experience some bereaved ladies managed initially to maintain an ultra-calm exterior only to suddenly break down into displays of wild grief - even throwing themselves about with great abandon. It would be more difficult, he hoped, for Mrs Myers to throw herself about while holding a cup of Horniman's finest Assam tea.

Also for the sake of informality he had accepted a slice of Madeira cake. He hated Madeira cake and was aware that coping with its crumbly texture, eating it, drinking the tea and conducting an interview might prove difficult.

Mrs Myers sensibly declined the Madeira cake, took a sip of tea then said, 'No-one, absolutely no-one. He was very much liked by his colleagues and friends as being trustworthy, reliable and honest.' She noticed that Best was waiting for something more so added, 'and he was kind. Very kind.'

She hadn't said loved. There was no mention of him being much loved. But perhaps her reserve prevented that or maybe she expected that to be taken as read. And she *was* referring to the esteem of his colleagues and friends not relatives.

He deliberately took a bite of the cake making immediate response impossible and left her answer hanging in the air for a few moments. Most women would not have been able to bear that silence. Would have felt obliged to fill it. Sometimes with a revealing remark.

But Mrs Myers was clearly not one of those. She waited calmly, straight-backed but not stiff, her fine eyes on him, until he had finished swallowing the cake, dabbed the crumbs from around his mouth, and taken another sip of tea to wash it down.

'I gathered from his acquaintances that Mr Myers was an honest man.' He paused. 'Always said what he thought.'

A faint, sad smile lit those fascinating eyes and struggled to lift the corners of her mouth.

'He did that all right. But not, I think, offensively so.'

Would she, he wondered, have seen the side of him which operated in the volatile world of politics or among the desperate at the dock gates? Unlikely.

His argument with Champion appeared to have been a heated one and the man insisted he had been verbally attacked by Myers. But then the survivor always had the last word.

'What I particularly liked about him,' she offered suddenly, 'was that he never pretended to be anything that he wasn't.'

Ah, the eternal middle-class obsession with the sin of trying to act above your station in life or, indeed, failing to live up what was judged to be your place in the world. This was obviously a very conventional lady. But clearly not so conventional as to refrain from marrying beneath her.

She looked about her. 'At first he was ill at ease here.'

Best followed her glance. It wasn't a particularly luxurious room. The furniture was all solid wood. None of that imitation wood veneer once so fashionable but now being attacked as a sign of vulgarity and bad taste not to mention also committing the sin of pretending to be something it was not.

None of the furniture appeared new, however. The sofa, armchairs, rocking chair and side tables showed some signs of wear although the luxurious draperies looked fresh and some of the knick-knacks and ornaments such as that French black marble mantel clock were probably more recently acquired. And as for that magnificent alabaster inkstand inlaid with sinuous flower forms - he had seen something like it being made by native craftsmen at last year's Colonial and Indian Exhibition.

He put down his cup and saucer with a sense of relief, wiped his mouth, hoping that no crumbs from that wretched Madeira cake were still clinging to his lips, and asked, 'When did you marry Mr Myers?'

'Three years ago.'

She closed her eyes.

Ah, now the reality was closing in. This time he hurried to fill the pause.

'I understand he was very involved with the SDF?'

She nodded. 'He cared a great deal about the iniquities heaped upon the working man.'

Best nodded and smiled. 'He was never tempted to join the ex-members in the Socialist League or the Fabians?'

'Oh, no. He thought they were too far removed from the working man.'

And Hyndman wasn't, thought Best?

She must have sensed his doubt and added. 'All that emphasis on education first when what was needed was action. Candidates put up for election and,' she smiled, 'keeping the government worried that there might be a revolution any moment.'

She regarded him curiously. Wondering why he should be so interested in political niceties when he was supposed to be investigating her husband's death? He sensed it was time to go. The burning question, 'Was he thinking of leaving you, Mrs Myers?' would have to be left to another time or be put to others who knew the man.

'Poor woman, widowed twice,' said Helen, pausing as she sorted out some of that day's sketches of the Reading Room at the British Museum, 'and losing the second one so quickly.'

Best nodded. 'Very sad.'

'You say she didn't seem terribly upset?'

'As far as I could tell. She was very controlled but I think, underneath that . . ' He frowned. 'There was something about her that was ... that was *different*.'

'In what way?'

She picked out four of the sketches and propped them up on the shelf that stretched alongside her studio wall.

He grimaced and shook his head. 'I don't know.'

'That's not like you.' She stood back to examine the chosen few. 'You're usually quite perceptive about people.' She turned her head towards him. 'Was it her appearance?'

'In a way.' He shook his head. 'But that's not exactly it - there was a mysterious aura about her.' He hesitated, 'It was as if she was a foreigner but wasn't - if you know what I mean?'

She laughed. 'No, my love, I don't!' She snatched two of the sketches away and put them to one side.

He knew that other men might resent some of their wife's attention being concentrated on their painting. But he didn't. It had been part of their pact. She loved him but would only agree to marry him if she could carry on with her work and not give it up as so many female artists were obliged to do once they married.

Besides, he enjoyed being part of it.

Before Helen the only outlet for his more flamboyant, artistic side had been his own attire. Some of his colleagues might consider his clothes a little too colourful but had to agree that his dark good looks allowed him to get away with them.

Their usefulness as a disguise, was, however, debatable and the subject which caused some disagreement among his superiors. At first sight no-one would ever suspect him to be a police officer and that was very useful. But, once seen, he was remembered, and *that* was not. But second time around he usually had the good sense either to tone down his appearance or to present a convincing enough alternative identity.

'You say she was very dark and 'smouldering', said Helen. 'Attractive, in a sinister sort of way?'

He shook his head in irritation at himself. 'Not *exactly* sinister - just - I don't know - *different*.

She took her attention from her work and looked at him. 'Could she be second generation Spanish for example? Spanish women are very good at that smouldering business. Or Italian perhaps?'

His mother was Italian as were many of his relatives but they did not seem mysterious like this woman.

'Not Italian,' he said, 'we don't smoulder.' He grinned and threw his arms in the air, 'We explode!'

'Hmph!' she groaned and raised her eyebrows. 'So dramatic.' She paused, had a thought and held up her right forefinger. 'Well then, how about her being a gypsy? One of those gypsies who has decided to cease roaming?'

Gypsy! Now that was an idea! Helen had sought out many of the gypsy women to draw when making illustrations of their Notting Dale encampment. Not that any *he* had come across had seemed very grand and mysterious. But might they do - if they were attempting to blend in with the English middle-classes?

'But would she speak so well?'

Helen shrugged, snatched up one of the two remaining drawings and said crisply. 'That can be learned. Don't forget the missionaries – and George Smith - have been down among them.'

George Smith, 'the Children's Friend', once a child labourer in a brickfield, had been educated by missionaries at night classes. He subsequently agitated to get education for brickyard children as well as those of the illiterate canal boatmen and now his attention had turned to the gypsy children.

Helen was a great admirer of his. Best had bumped into Smith when he was obliged to join a canal boat crew while investigating a murder on the Regent's Canal; the case on which he and Helen had met.

She was right. Mrs Myers could be a gypsy. It fitted. Almost, anyway.

'You should go back a little later when she has had more time to adjust to being widowed yet again. This mysteriousness may just be sorrow.'

'I will. I will. Meanwhile, I'll make some more enquiries about her.'

Helen had been moving from side to side viewing the remaining sketch from every angle. Now she wrinkled her nose critically and lifted her shoulders. Not happy. It looked splendid to Best but he knew that now was not a time to comment.

'If you can, get the opinion of another woman.' She looked at him, head on one side. 'Of course, if she is so attractive. . .' She paused. 'You know what that means?'

'Exactly,' he sighed. 'Another motive for murder.'

11

Albert was disappointed. The calling foremen at the London Dock had not picked him out. But then they had not picked out many other men either. There had been little work on offer that morning.

Only two contract men had come to the dock gates, shouted out a few names from their registers, selected one or two familiar young faces and left the rest standing.

Some of those not taken on left immediately to try for work at the other docks. Others, including Albert, stood around until they were allowed into the waiting yard, the holding bay for the ever-hopeful, where they sat on long benches ranged against the wall and shared their misery, stared into space or dozed.

Albert soon learned from Jerry, a runtish, pimply young man sitting to his right, that some of those who had left would be trying their luck at the Surrey Docks on the South side of the river. Baltic ships carrying bacon and Canadian vessels loaded with grain and timber came in there.

Some would go to stand on Tower Bridge where banks were in view and they could see if there was a new boat coming in anywhere.

So that his questions would not seem strange Albert had made it plain that he was a greenhorn and Jerry seemed happy to alleviate his own boredom by taking on the role of teacher. Fortunately, Jerry was not in the least curious about Albert who was mindful of Best's instruction not to reveal too much about himself. If personal revelations were called for he should stick to his fictitious background. He was an out of work navvy.

As they talked he began to feel spots of rain on his face and quickly leaned back under the eaves of a warehouse roof. Not only would his threadbare clothes quickly get soaked but his flour and soot makeup may become strangely streaky.

He took his time before getting around to asking about the calling foremen.

When he did the response was like a flash flood.

Jerry, whose delivery had up to then been laconic and toneless, came alive. There was fire in his eyes and some colour even leached into his sallow, spotty cheeks as, counting them off on his fingers, he launched into a run down on their various peccadillos.

'Jones,'e doesn't like foreigners, Wilson, that one likes to see you scrambling on the ground for your pass and Arthur, he's a decent bloke, used to be one of us'. He paused his expression growing angry and his eyes hurt as he described Henderson. 'That one is a sadist. Likes dangling you like a fish.' Jerry's fists balled. 'He'll pick you out and you'll go forward for your pass then he'll change his mind, shake his head and brush you off.'

Albert shook his head in disbelief at the cruelties of this world. 'Terrible. Terrible.' Then, after a respectful lull, ventured casually, "Ere, what about that one that got hisself murdered?'

Several of the other waiting men, who up to that moment had been disinterested in furthering Albert's education, were suddenly alert when Jerry exclaimed, '*That* one! I could tell you a thing or two about *that* one!'

'But that's excellent!' Best exclaimed when faced with the crestfallen Albert, who was quite sure that he had failed utterly and was convinced his career as a budding detective was over before it had begun.

He had not only failed to get taken on but also failed to extract the 'thing or two' hinted at by Jerry because the other men had silenced him with their warning glances.

'Don't you see,' enthused Best. 'Not only did you get in among them without arousing suspicion but you found out that there *is* something to learn. There may be a motive 'or two' hidden there. And *not* getting taken on will help you to seem genuine.

Albert was quite nonplussed by Best's enthusiasm which was, in truth, somewhat exaggerated for his benefit. But not entirely. It *was* progress of a kind, Best felt. Indeed the only progress so far. Hadn't he learned from that old warhorse Cheadle that even when one line of enquiry came to a dead end that was progress.

'It narrows the frame, laddie,' he would say. 'Narrows the frame. Makes you look harder at other parts of the picture, don't it?' Cheadle and his pictures.

And in fact this news, that there *was* something to be revealed by these casual dock labourers, had narrowed the frame – if only a little.

'It'll come out now,' Best insisted. 'Just keep at it.'

* * *

His new duties at the London docks did mean that Albert was nearer to Florence but he was still not close enough to protect her. He fretted about her safety not only with regards to Stark but also the Skeleton Army and others who attacked the Salvation Army marches and meetings by spitting, throwing sticks, stones, flour, rotting vegetables and even punches.

Some assailants who thought of themselves as devout had genuine objections to the Army's noisy and presumptive way of exhibiting (there was no other way of putting it, they said) their religious beliefs. They insulted the Lord with their brass bands, Moody and Sankey hymns, and popular music hall tunes.

Neither was the army's constant harping on about temperance appreciated by the working classes. After all, a drink in a warm and cheerful pub, was one of the few enjoyments in their hard and drab lives.

Of course some who attacked them were merely looking for a fight. A battle in which they were unlikely to get hurt was an even more attractive proposition. These Soldiers of the Lord were not only forbidden to strike back but were offered little protection from the authorities. Indeed, it was often they who were arrested for inciting the public disorder with their illegal marches and inflammatory preaching – even by women! Women in uniform, no less!

However, in London at least, things had begun to change just a little. Had they not, Albert and Florence might never have met.

It had all began one day when Albert was told to be outside a Salvation Army meeting hall on his beat in Stoke Newington so as to prevent disorder when the corps returned after one of their outdoor services.

This was a tall order but Albert was fearsomely big and strong. Accompanying the marchers on this occasion were almost as many Skeleton Army roughs.

No-one was quite sure how the Skeleton Army got its name. There were several theories. As for who organised them there was a strong suspicion that they were encouraged and even financed by the publicans and breweries who feared that their customers might just begin to listen to the dramatic warnings about the evils of the demon drink.

That day, the roughs followed the corps into the meeting hall and pandemonium broke out. Albert was called in to sort it out. He did so, with gusto. His decisive actions were even reported with wide-eyed wonder by a reporter from a national newspaper - much to the chagrin of senior officers. But Albert, after submitting the required report which a more educated and devious friend helped him compose, survived that trial.

Henceforth the local Salvationists always requested police protection when marching and were allotted a constable to guard them and this constable often turned out to be Albert. Being conscious of the fact that there would be times when even his superior strength and pugilistic prowess would prove insufficient to protect them and himself, he fashioned a secret weapon.

He acquired a short length of old rubber tyre from a cabbie and attached to it a length of catapult elastic which he slipped up his sleeve and tied to his braces.

Whenever he was in danger of being overwhelmed by thugs he would stretch his arm out sharply then retract it equally quickly so that the length of rubber tyre shot out and smacked the aggressor on the chin before being quickly withdrawn.

To say they did not know what hit them would be an understatement. They would gaze around in startled and dazed confusion. Sometimes Albert could not resist telling them, 'The Lord is on our side!' which caused the Army to imagine they had a convert.

Best would have been surprised to learn that Albert *could* keep some secrets and this was one of them.

Marching with the corps along Stoke Newington High Street on the fateful day he noticed that members of the Skeleton Army were up to one of their usual tricks - marching towards them in a wide column. They knew the Salvation Army would not cut and run so they would keep marching, infiltrate their ranks, attack officers, rip their drums and seize their cornets and trumpets.

And this is what happened on the day Albert met his fate. He went on the offensive just as the Skeleton Army were getting started. He instantly felled two of the ringleaders which caused some momentary confusion in their ranks. But they regrouped and began to attack again. One of their victims was a tiny young Sally who fell to the ground as her bonnet was ripped from her head and her tambourine torn from her hand.

Outraged, Albert roared in, used his secret weapon on one man, an uppercut on another and literally threw a third, who was approaching fast, right across the road.

Then he reached down to help the fallen Hallelujah Lass to her feet. She glanced up at him, gratitude in her china blue eyes, a tremulous smile on her pretty pink lips and Albert fell instantly in love.

From then on, it was understood that Albert, and only Albert, was to escort the marches. In his usual confiding manner he had revealed his lovelorn plight to his colleagues and they felt obliged to help him make this girl, Florence, his own even though she was a member of an organisation which caused them so much trouble.

News of his progress in the love stakes, slow at first, was followed avidly by his colleagues. When he finally won through the warm glow of satisfaction was shared by all.

12

'Decoyed or strayed. Decoyed or strayed.' Florence couldn't get the words out of her head. They chilled her to the bone and filled her mind with dreadful scenes.

When she had finished her duties at the Army's Rescue Centre she had taken little Mary Phillcocks's description with her:

Dark blue eyes with a slight cross, brown hair, a rather thin face, height about 3ft 9inches, mark on the thigh.

She had it now as she left home, the bare room she shared with Annie Cartwright, a fellow officer, in Bethnal Green. She was heading for duty back in Whitechapel, outside the Royal Cambridge Music Hall in Commercial Street.

On her way she searched the faces of little girls selling matches or boot-laces, or just holding out their grimy palms and tilting their pathetic faces beseechingly.

Were any of them 3ft 9inches tall? She found it difficult to judge despite having measured that height against the rescue centre wall. She decided just to look for girls who seemed to be about ten or eleven years of age. An East End ten or eleven year old that is. Children who had regular meals and were not obliged to work, were, of course, taller, plumper and showed none of the strain she saw on the pinched faces of their poorer counterparts.

In the fading light she found it hard to tell whether any of the little girls had dark blue eyes with a slight cross but as the kerbside costers began to turn on their naphtha lamps her task became easier.

Brown hair? Who could tell the colour of filthy, matted hair?

A mark on the thigh? Looking out the actual letter from Mary's parents she had discovered that the mark was in fact a dark oval birthmark with a little tail giving it the appearance of a teardrop. But she could scarcely ask children to show her their thighs. She decided, however, that she would do just that if she was convinced that a child could be Mary Phillcocks whose mother thought she had been decoyed or had strayed.

It suddenly occurred to her how strange it was that while Mary's 'heartbroken' parents were not sure whether their daughter was ten or eleven years of age they reported her height as a precise 3ft 9inches?

Thin. They said she was thin. But most of the children who thronged the pavements and gutters here were pitifully thin, some to the point of being gaunt due to starvation. It was heart-breaking to examine them so closely and to see their dulled faces light up when they thought she was going to buy their wares or place a coin in their outstretched hands.

She wanted to but that would leave no money for food for her home calls and for food for herself and Annie. Mrs Booth had warned them again that if they starved themselves to give to others they risked becoming too weak to serve the Lord.

Albert was fond of pointing out that General Booth and his wife Catherine lived in a very nice house in a very nice neighbourhood and had more than enough to eat. He was sure that they (or rather their servants) did not have to search through Francatellis *Plain Cookery Book for the Working Classes* to find the cheapest possible dishes. No cow-heel broth and 'Economical and Substantial Soup for Distribution to the Poor' for them.

He believed what some of their enemies claimed, that the Skeleton Army had so dubbed themselves to mock half-starved Salvationists - mostly female Salvationists. The women were not only paid less than their male counterparts but were required to serve on the Gutter, Cellar and Garret Brigade, work not thought not proper for the men to do.

But Albert did not understand. It was important that the General and Mrs Booth kept up their strength and were not distracted by mundane matters from their work which was to lead.

She made her way along Whitechapel Road pavements crowded with shoppers and idle promenaders. Some were shabby, some quite well dressed, all were harangued by the costers' bellows.

'Plaice alive! Alive! Cheap!'

She leaped back in fright as two lads bellowed into her face in unison, 'Pineapples ha'penny a slice! Pineapple ha'penny a slice!'

To save their own voice costers would employ young urchins to shout in concert, and they got great sport out of it.

Disturbed by the sudden blast of noise she hurried on past groups of people eating or waiting in front of the whelk and baked potato stalls or congregating outside the pubs.

Now and then she stopped and even got down on her hands and knees to peer at homeless children huddled in doorways of the few shuttered shops. any who looked promising she woke up. But none were Mary.

Those she disturbed she gave one the stale buns donated by her local Belgian baker won over by her pretty, earnest face. She tried to persuade the children to go to their rescue home or to Dr Barnardos. But no matter how cold and hungry they usually refused preferring freedom. She knew that some of them would drift in when the nights grew colder - if they survived till then.

All at once just ahead of her, hoisted on the shoulders of a big, bushy-haired man, was a little girl with an oval birthmark on her thigh!

The man was walking fast. The little girl had to hang on to his hair to keep her balance. Florence almost broke into a run to keep up with him. She had to see the child from the front. She had almost caught up when a crowd, spilling out from the King Harry's Arms, blocked her path. Several men tried to detain her with chaff about the Sallies. Some were friendly. Some not.

By the time she had pushed her way through them the big man had gone. If only she'd had the courage to stop him! She started to run. People stared and looked behind her to see who might be in pursuit and exchanged puzzled glances when they saw no-one.

At a side street she was almost knocked down by a rag and bone cart turning in from the main road. The driver swore after her furiously making her blush as she ran. She wished she didn't do that! So often, when she was trying to appear imperturbable. The colour would creep up from her neck or, as in this case, just flash across her face.

She was about to give up when she caught sight of the big man just ahead of her in front of a sweet stall. The child had been lowered to the ground the better to choose from the wares: shiny black balls, sticky almond toffee, dark treacle rock and gaudy lollipops.

After some serious deliberation she chose a red and white striped halfpenny lollipop. Florence edged around her to catch a glimpse of her eyes but they remained fixed on the contents of the barrow.

She did manage to see her hair peeping out of the sides of her bonnet.

It was black. Quite black. No mistaking that and the eyes when she finally turned them Florence's way were not dark blue but dark brown, almost black too.

Florence's stares began to draw attention. Feeling quite foolish, she turned away quickly and continued on towards the south end of Commercial Street. She had made herself late looking for the child so she spent some precious pennies on a tram ride up to the Royal Cambridge Theatre.

By the time she arrived the theatre doors had been opened and some eying-up and tentative bartering with the prostitutes around the entrance had already begun.

Although large, the Royal Cambridge showed a plainer face to the world than many of its competitors. To draw in customers it relied instead on bright posters, a couple of lofty Grecian columns on either side of the entrance and a hall beyond lit by twinkling ornamental stars suspended from the ceiling.

The theatre was a favourite with some of the young bucks from the West End who enjoyed first sampling the turns at the rumbustious East London Music Hall and afterwards – or in between the performances - partaking of the fleshly charms of the young women outside.

The buildings' lack of fashionable ornamentation was of no concern to them. What they liked was its situation: within the exciting and dangerous East End - but not too far in. The appropriately seedy Spitalfields was at the end of the highway which led from the docks to the wholesale markets of the City of London. Escape back west was quick and easy.

She recognised two of the men gathered by the alleyway leading to the stage door. She knew who they were and what they were doing. They were chirrupers hoping to catch the artistes as they dashed in and promise, if rewarded, to greet their acts with roars of applause. If no money was forthcoming they threatened to ruin their performances with a barrage of jeers and catcalls.

Florence was still capable of being amazed by the wickedness in the world. I must tell Albert about this, she thought. It was blackmail and that was against the law.

While she was approaching the young prostitutes Florence's attention kept being drawn towards the Peabody Buildings opposite, the place from which young Mary Phillcocks had strayed or been decoyed. She determined to go there in between curtain up and her regular home calls.

When the first house commenced she began to cross the street avoiding the eye of a drunken woman who had been standing outside a gin shop with the baby in her arms and who had now begun wobbling towards her.

Florence ignored her, hoping the Lord would forgive her. The woman probably wanted to sell her baby for a few pence to buy more gin – or maybe even give it away.

I'll get it tomorrow night, she told herself, and take it to the Baby Home. I must go to see Mary's parents now. She didn't know why but she felt it was urgent. That she had to go right now. But she did.

*   *   *

It was then that he saw her. At first he was not certain that the small, neat, bonneted figure in Salvation Army uniform was the same one he had been searching for. These sanctimonious, interfering busybodies with their provocative ways were not an unusual sight in this area and he had followed several of them, hoping.

But the way she held herself very upright made him almost sure. This time it *was* her. As she turned her head each way to watch the traffic before crossing Commercial Street her pretty little features were illuminated by the lights of the pub on the corner. Yes! It was her!

At last he had found her. He felt a surge of triumph. He shook his fists and clenched his teeth in anticipation. They must have moved her around so he could not find her. But now he had and this time she would not escape.

He grinned to himself. He knew how these Hallelujah Lasses were instructed to face imminent danger: 'Fall on your knees and pray'.

Excellent. Like a lamb to the slaughter.

He couldn't wait.

13

Florence felt even more guilty for ignoring the woman with the baby when she admitted to herself that she had another reason for visiting Peabody Buildings apart from an unauthorised visit to Mary's parents.

Her inclination to act impulsively and difficulty with obeying rules was not new. It was these traits which had resulted in her joining the Salvation Army in defiance of her bullying father.

She believed wholeheartedly in the cause but was also eager to get away from that domineering man who called *her* an unnatural woman for her wilfulness. Thank goodness Albert was not like him. He respected her decisions and her work.

It was Albert – or at least their life together – which was her other reason for visiting these model dwellings. She wanted to see what they were like inside and what kind of people lived there.

She knew that these were the first Peabody Buildings to be built in London and had been meant for the poor but that it had turned out that the poor could not afford the four or five shillings a week rent. Consequently, they had been let to skilled workmen, mechanics, and policemen and their families.

Her duty visits were to the homes of the very poor who lived in squalid courts and filthy alleys. She had never had the need to visit any of the new model dwellings being erected all over Whitechapel and Spitalfields.

That was going to change. She intended to visit all of them – or at least *most* of them - to find a suitable home for her and Albert when they were married.

Some found the monumental facade of these Peabody Buildings forbidding. The five-story yellow-brown block rose sheer from the pavement almost like the prow of a ship. But Florence was undeterred. It was what they were like inside that mattered.

When she got closer she noticed that there had been an effort to break up the plain front with red brick decoration and cream trims and, of course there was a row of useful shops at ground level.

Perhaps she was looking at them with rose-coloured spectacles, as her father was always accusing her of doing. But even he would have had to concede that the location of these tenements could not be more suitable for her and Albert.

Not only was there a splendid new police station just up the street but her own 'beat' was close by. And right next door was the marvellous Spitalfields Market where they could buy their food cheaply. What's more, Albert would feel right at home here having been born and brought up nearby. What could be better?

Providing they were clean and pleasant enough inside the monumental Peabody Buildings were, she decided cheerfully, *exactly* what they needed.

Should they disappoint she would inspect the others on her viewing list such as the East London Dwellings Company blocks in Goulston and Wentworth Streets and the Charlotte de Rothschild's Dwellings in Thrawle and Flower and Dean Streets.

She might even look at the Jewish and East London Model Lodgings, further down Commercial Street. They, she had discovered, were obliged to accept a certain number of non-Jewish tenants. Of course, she would avoid those tenements which had been jerry built and were already falling into disrepair and becoming the haunts of criminals.

But it was the location of these Peabody Buildings which made them the favourite. Albert was unaware of her quest. That was going to be a surprise.

She smiled in anticipation of his approval. Sometimes he accused her of not wanting to get married as much as he did because she was to taken up with her Army duties. This would show him differently.

She was grateful that, unlike the boyfriends of some of her colleagues, he never tried to get her to give up her calling. Some boyfriends were embarrassed by the army's reputation. Some, Florence thought, were just jealous of the attention their girlfriends gave to the movement.

She walked past by the row of shops stopping by the Superintendent's office at their centre and rang the bell. He directed her to the entrance around the corner in White Lion Street.

Would one of the flats above the shops suit, she wondered as she walked by them? Or would they be too noisy? A lot of heavy traffic from the docks passed up Commercial Street. She wished Albert was here so they could talk about it but there had been little chance of even a brief meeting lately what with her duties and his twelve hour shifts.

As she turned into dimly-lit White Lion Street the first wisps of fog were beginning to creep along the ground. The stairways, on the interior side of the building, were open to the elements as were the corridors and fog had begun stealing its way along those too.

The Phillcocks lived on the second landing at number nineteen. A small, apologetic, bird-like woman opened the door and to her surprise quickly beckoned Florence in and closed it before she had even had time to explain the purpose of her visit.

'Keep out the cold air and fog,' she explained 'and prying eyes.' Florence could see the problem. The front door opened from the living room directly onto the open landing. There was no interior corridor or lobby to shield the occupants from the outside elements or protect their privacy. What would Albert think about that?

Ida Phillcocks showed no surprise at Florence's visit but immediately sat her down before the large lovingly black-leaded fire range.

'We've told the police,' she said, tugging at the handkerchief balled up in her hand. 'They said they'd keep an eye out for Mary and look in the places we said,' she went on eagerly. Then she stopped and looked at Florence sadly, 'But you know what it's like.'

Florence did. So many children loose on the streets. Some sent out to earn money, sometimes by drunken or merely desperate parents. Some deciding to stay there, a draughty doorway being preferable to a beating from an inebriate father especially if they had failed to earn enough money. Then there were the homeless orphans dodging missionaries and others who tried to tempt them into workhouses or orphanages. Others, too, who had been decoyed by less well-meaning persons.

Decoyed into brothels, being passed off as above the legal age of twelve – as if the customers cared. Or worse into the hands of some evil child molester.

There were so many stray children out there. The police had little hope of finding one in this haystack and usually didn't bother too much, particularly now they had so many other problems on their hands. Poor little Mary Phillcocks had little chance of being noticed by them.

'Joe's out there now, looking for her. He goes out every night after work an' I look in the daytime.' She shook her head. 'But we ain't found her.'

'Was there any reason she might have wanted to run away?' Florence asked feeling a bit out of her depth. Was she doing any good here? She had no experience of this sort of thing. Albert would know what to ask. She wished he was here.

'Had she been told off for being naughty or . . .anything like that?' she added lamely.

'Oh, no. No! the woman shook her head emphatically. 'She was very happy at home. We sent her to school and ... and we didn't beat her or nothing like that.'

As tears threatened Florence changed tack.

When she ran out of questions Florence glanced around the cosy room and said, 'You've got this place very nice.'

The woman warmed to the compliment. She was clearly pleased just to have someone to talk to.

'We was very happy when we got it.' She pointed to the bare brick walls which had been painted a cedar green, 'We'd like to be able to put up wallpaper but that's not allowed.' She shrugged. 'But they do give us the paint and that.'

Florence could see the reason for the rule. Wallpaper harboured bugs and dirt and germs but they could have softened the rough bricks and mortar with a coat of plaster. Then again, it was still a lot better than where *she* was living now.

'Are any of these flats vacant?' she asked, then blushed guiltily. Ida didn't seem to notice.

'Oh, yes. There's one above us. An old boy has just died and his missus is going to live with her daughter.' She pointed to the ceiling and looked at her quizzically.

Florence came clean in a rush. 'It was just,' she said, 'that I'm getting married soon to a policeman and I thought this might suit us being so near a police station and to where I work.'

The woman beamed when she said this and Florence saw how she must have looked before losing her child.

'Oh, he'll be in good company! Quite a few police families live here already.'

That opened the floodgates. Florence was given a potted run-down on the advantages and disadvantages of living in the Spitalfields Peabody Buildings. Most of the neighbours were respectable working people like mechanics, policemen and clerks. Costermongers could afford them but didn't want them because there were rules against subletting and there was nowhere to put their barrows.

The chief drawback, it seemed, was keeping out the cold air and warming the bedrooms which had no fireplaces. The lavatories, washhouses, and dust shoots were all very clean and efficient but were right at the ends of the open corridors.

'And it can be a bit cold getting to them in the winter,' said Ida rubbing her upper arms in demonstration.

So, some good things and some not so good but, she reminded herself, it was still better than where she lived now and better than Albert's Section House where he had to sleep in a cubicle and was woken at night by the chimes of Big Ben just across the road.

Despite the fact that she had been of no help in finding Mary the woman seemed reluctant to let her go.

'I have to do my rounds,' Florence apologised. 'But I'll come again and keep looking out for Mary.'

As she stood up to go the question which had been hovering irritatingly at the back of her mind suddenly sprang forward.

'Oh, I couldn't help wondering why, I thought it a little strange.' How could she put this? Straightforwardly her Captain always insisted. 'Why you knew Mary's height so precisely but were not sure of her age?'

Ida went white and stared at her.

'Oh, don't tell me if you don't want to,' Florence said floundering. 'I just wanted to know as much as possible so that . . .'

'*She* didn't know how old she was,' Ida broke in tremulously,

Florence frowned. 'I don't understand, I mean when she was born . . .'

'She wasn't always ours. We found her on the street,' said Ida, tears spilling. 'An now she's gone back there.'

Why was she spending so long in there? What was she doing? Couldn't be one of her usual calls. He sighed. Never mind, I can wait, he thought. The fog was really thick now. She wouldn't be able to see him when she came out. The puny street lights were scarcely pinpricks.

At first he had been angry that she had not gone to a lonely alley or a murky courtyard and horrified that she had chosen this particular address.

What did she know? He shrugged. Well soon it wouldn't matter. The street was normally fairly busy but the fog, thickening by the minute, was sending people indoors and that suited him just fine. He wouldn't *need* a dark court or alley. He fingered the blade in his pocket and waited.

14

Florence shivered as she left the flat and made her way down the open staircase. She should have worn her cloak and not minded about appearing too 'official'.

She had noticed the misty tendrils creeping up the staircase but was unprepared for the solid wall of fog which greeted her when she reached the street.

It brought her up sharp, clinging around her, shutting out her senses. She felt as if she had instantaneously become blind and deaf. She stopped to take stock. It was so easy to get lost in a fog. But the traffic sounds of Commercial Street now dimmed, deadened and other-worldly, were in reality she knew, no distance away on her left.

She turned towards them and began feeling her way along the tenement wall. Then she stopped abruptly. Someone was close by. She was sure of it. She could sense them.

'Whose there?' she said trying to keep the fear from her voice.

No reply. She listened hard. Was that someone breathing! Then it came - the smell! Underlying the familiar sulphureous whiff of fog there was another faint odour - and it was familiar. One she would never forget. She froze, terror gripping her.

She knows I'm here, he thought, waiting in her path, and the idea pleased him. Serve her right. And his eyes and senses were more adjusted than hers. He was prepared. But, in any case clear vision not really necessary. She was walking straight into his net like a fly into a spider's web. He pulled back the hand which was holding the knife. She was short. Keep it low. With luck it would go right into her heart. He sighed. At last, an end to his problem. One of these interfering, sanctimonious uniformed women wanting to interfere in his pleasures.

She forced herself to move again. She couldn't stand here all night. She was imagining things. Conjuring up that smell out of fear. But it was getting stronger! She stopped again. If only Albert was here! What should she do? She was supposed to trust in the Lord and feel no fear. But she did! She did!

She would turn around. That's what she would do. Go the other way. Go back into Peabody Buildings. That was it! That was it! She began to turn. Was that an intake of breath she heard! It was too late! There was someone right in front of her – she could hear his heavy breathing now and see his shadowy form! Then the scrape heavy boots and another figure to the side. Two of them! A dazzling light shone into her face, blinding her. Oh my God, protect me! Please, protect me!

'Here, Miss,' said a loud voice in her ear. His hand was on her arm. 'You shouldn't be out saving souls on a night like this!'

Florence tried to speak but could only croak and then a whisper, 'My calls...'

"No good trying to do them tonight, Miss. It's coming down worse all the time. Best go home now.'

The police sergeant held his lantern forward to light her uncertain steps. She was shaking and trying not to cry.

'Let's get you to the corner where the light's better, then I'll have one of my men see you home. Don't worry. Your flock will still be there tomorrow.'

Florence still couldn't speak as they moved forward alongside the wall. There was no-one there now and the smell had gone too.

'I'm sure that General of yours wouldn't want you to get yourself killed. Fogs this bad are dangerous, you know. Especially round here. Just going on duty, myself,' said the sergeant companionably. 'Be a busy night in the hospitals and the morgues I can tell you.'

'I'd like to get Florence away from them,' announced Albert.

Best frowned. 'Why? She's devoted to the Salvation Army?'

'Well, it's dangerous for a start, isn't it? Look at that woman in Chester.'

A Salvation Army Captain in Chester had been struck on the head by a large stone when her division had marched through the City's Irish quarter. According to the newspapers her condition was now 'exciting considerable anxiety.'

'And then there's that Stark business.'

'He wouldn't dare touch her,' insisted Best with more conviction than he felt.

Albert was unconvinced. 'It's worrying me to death.'

'She knows she has to be careful.'

'I wish she did. She seems to have no fear.'

'I expect she feels the Lord will protect her.'

Albert made a hurrumping sound. 'Like he was doing when we met?'

'Yes,' laughed Best. 'He sent you to save her, didn't he?'

Albert glanced skywards in disgust. 'No. It was my inspector what sent me.'

'Ah, but who told him to?' Best teased and paused. 'You don't believe in divine intervention?'

He shook his head. 'Nah. I'm one of Florence's "unsaved souls".'

'Well, one thing you have to admit. If she hadn't have been a Hallelujah Lass you would never have met her.'

Albert grunted and admitted with a rueful grimace, 'I suppose that's true.'

That fact duly acknowledged they turned their attention back to the huddled inhabitants of Trafalgar Square who were trying to keep warm on this damp and chilly night.

'Tell you one thing,' Albert admitted as they surveyed the throng, 'I'm glad I was down at the docks when all that business was going on here. She'd have given me some stick for that!'

Several days earlier, unruly crowds, sporting red and black banners and holding Liberty caps aloft had gathered in the square and marched to the City of London to confront the Lord Mayor again then marched back again to Trafalgar Square. Warren, in response to criticism about lack of action, took some. He had the square cleared.

Much mayhem and many arrests followed along with accusations of police brutality though the police themselves did not emerge un-bloodied.

Many of the crowd simply moved, as on other previous occasions, to Hyde Park where they continued with their meetings, but attempts to resume marching across the city were blocked. They responded with stones and crowbars and accusations that the police were betraying their brothers. They were met, uncompromisingly, with fists and truncheons.

One night, while the daytime inhabitants were still being kept out, several hundred of the night habitués were allowed into the square but after midnight were confronted by policemen armed with Casual Ward admission tickets. If they refused them and failed to disperse they could be charged under the Vagrancy Act with being without fixed abode.

Since then, there had been another abrupt change of tactics. The daytime 'mob' were allowed back in the square. Indeed, had marched back escorted by the police, much to their disgust and that of many of the public particularly the shopkeepers who feared for their livelihoods.

However, due to the recent showers and a sharp north-easterly wind, the nightly numbers of homeless were somewhat diminished. Some were taking refuge in less exposed places, under arches or in doorways. Others had accepted the hated option of the workhouse.

'What d'you think?' said Albert.

'I think it's a pity that someone can't give them some work – those that want it of course.' Not all did. The undeserving poor some called them and much worse but the Salvation Army leader, General Booth, claimed there was no such thing. They were all deserving.

'No, I mean about Florence.'

Ah, Albert casting around for answers to his problems. Others, Best knew, would be similarly canvassed.

'Should I try to get her to give it up? Tell her that when we are married ...'

Best shook his head firmly. He always tried to resist giving Albert the advice he solicited not wanting to encourage this habit in someone who might need to make instant life-preserving decisions one day. But, such was the lad's eager charm and his endearing need, he too often succumbed.

'I think you'd just drive her away if you did that.'

'My dad says I should put my foot down.'

Best almost laughed out loud.

Albert was putty in Florence's hands and the idea of him acting the typical East End husband *was* laughable. Best had a wilful wife of his own. One of the new breed. So he understood the problem.

'You'll have to use a bit of native cunning,' he said, tapping the side of his nose.

'Oh, yes?' Albert waited eagerly.

'Instead of trying to persuade her out of it – which would only cause bad feeling – get married as soon as you can. Then try to get posted to a station as far as possible from the East End.' He paused and smiled. 'Anyway, when she starts having babies she won't have the time to go out with the Cellar, Gutter and Garret Brigade, will she?'

'Was that how it worked for you?'

'In a way,' Best lied. 'In a way.'

He refrained from explaining what it had really been like for them: Helen refusing to marry him unless she could carry on painting and that in between there had been much tragedy, heartache and compromise. The lad was confused enough.

Albert shrugged disconsolately. 'I think she'll be hard to move.'

There was no answer to that so Best just murmured that things could change and that you never knew what was around the corner.

Albert turned his attention to Best's problems and what he regarded as 'their case'. Best described his meeting at the SDF headquarters in Parliament Square.

'I think there's more to this split than they are letting on.' He shrugged. 'I suppose I'd better go and see Mr Morris and his Socialist League members. Find out what they have to say.'

'Why don't you speak to my friend Alec Burns first?'

'Alec Burns the boxer?' Best furrowed his brow.

'That's him. Used to be my room mate in the section house. Taught me how to box.'

Best frowned, 'Wasn't he . . ?'

'Chucked out of the Force? Yeh. For accepting a two shilling tip. Very hard that was.'

'Why should I speak to him?'

'He's John Burns's brother.'

'Oh? I didn't know that!' John Burns was a fiery SDF member who had been trying to spur the police into revolt about their conditions.

'Would he speak to me?'

'Yeh, for his old pal.'

'Splendid.'

Albert grinned. He had helped with their case. He might become a detective yet.

15

The docks were the most exciting place in London, thought Albert, as he was marched along bustling quaysides behind a calling foreman. Probably the most exciting in the world.

He knew that few Londoners were able to see these fascinating places. The Thames river front with its immense warehouses and factories presented a barrier like tall trees on the edge of a jungle. Behind them lurked the hinterland, or in this case, numerous enclosed docks.

Even those living and working around them glimpsed only the tallest masts and funnels peeping over their high brick walls. Only if they actually worked there would they witness the arrival of tea from Ceylon, ivory and camels from Africa, paper from Newfoundland, oils, essences and dried monkey skins from Zanzibar, carpets from Turkey, Persia, Afghanistan and China, timber from Canada, elephants from India and sugar from Trinidad. All the local inhabitants saw was the constant traffic carrying these goods out and clogging up their roads.

Indeed, the only inkling most Londoner got of all this frantic world-wide commerce was the view down river from London or Tower Bridge where ships might be seen queuing to be let in through the locks and channels or being unloaded onto barges by lightermen.

The foreman was walking at such a pace that Albert scarcely had time to absorb all the exciting sights, sounds and frantic activity.

His new friend Jerry had not been chosen by the calling foreman which made Albert feel guilty that he had and also sorry that he had lost an important contact.

But soon Albert's ready grin and endearing habit of sharing his problems won the help of two of the other chosen men, curly-headed Freddie and toothless but wiry Enoch.

The problem that he shared with these two men was a genuine one. He didn't know what he was doing and was anxious that his ignorance might cause him to stand out.

'That might stop me getting more work,' he explained.

He did not yet realise that his fellow workmen might be reluctant to offer advice. Indeed be happy to see him go under. He was a competitor in this fearful game and might, particularly being strong young man, later take the bread from their mouths. But Albert's open manner and innocent blue eyes reminded Freddie of his younger brother, Archie. His late younger brother, dead of tuberculosis at nineteen.

Albert had imagined going down into the holds of these ships from exciting foreign parts to unload their exotic cargo or fill them up with much admired British manufactured goods for their return journey across the world.

But, it transpired, these tasks were skilled and were also for stevedores, permanent men, who knew how to load a craft so that it did not become unbalanced and capsize and place the goods in the right order for unloading at various ports. Unloading, too, apparently required their practised hands and eyes which knew how to place chains around awkward boxes and give the right signals to the crane operators to lift them up and over to the dockside.

It was only when the bales, crates and barrels had been piled up on the dockside that the casuals took over. They 'trucked' it to the warehouses on barrows. A seemingly simple task but one requiring a great deal of strength and energy. The loads they were expected to balance and carry, Albert discovered, were large, heavy, often unwieldy and had to be moved fast, very fast – almost at a run. No wonder Myers had a stopwatch – their runs were timed and if they weren't fast enough they were ditched!

By the time they lowered their barrows for a short break Albert was exhausted. Before they could even contemplate their food they had to get back their breaths and strength. Once they did, Albert was horrified to see Freddie unwrap his bundle to reveal a mean scrap of stale bread and a morsel of cheese. In his, bundle were two large ham sandwiches and two pork sausages. He wanted to give one of the sandwiches to Freddie but was not sure how to go about it. Would the he be offended? Or even suspicious?

In the end he first told a tale of how he had cheekily lifted the ham from an outside a butcher's display last night and had already eaten rather too much of it for breakfast.

'You'd better help me out here. Daren't take any home or she'll start up at me again about stealing!'

Freddie, whose eyes had not left the bulging sandwiches took little persuading.

'Makes you ache this work, don't it?' said Albert rubbing his arms and shoulder and abandoning his attempts at proper English in a good cause.

Freddie was gobbling the sandwich down quickly, as if he was afraid Albert might change his mind and take it back. He swallowed, looking slightly embarrassed, and nodded.

'Aye. Specially if you ain't done it before. 'And,' he glanced down at the food in his grimy fist, 'it brings on a terrible hunger.' He looked away angrily. 'Then the bugger is, if you don't get enough to eat you're too bloody skinny and weak to do it any more and they won't take you on!'

Albert could truthfully say that he had never worked so hard. No doubt standing on his feet for twelve hours a day in all weathers was very tiring but this was worse, much worse - and all for only five pence an hour - when you could get it.

'Not so bad as sugar though. Don't do sugar unless you have to. Rough to handle that. Makes you bleed.'

It appeared that sacks of sugar, which were unloaded in large quantities down the road at the North Quay of the West India Docks, was not only bloody heavy but the granules from the leaking sacks got onto your skin and dug in as you worked and scraped it until you bled.

'That's why they call it Blood Alley.'

Albert made an eager listener to their tales about the docks. They told him about the cosy and old fashioned St Katherine's, the gloomy West India, the impressive new Royal twins the Victoria and Albert and the awe-inspiring complicated miles of the Surrey Commercial on the South side of the river with its rafts of floating timber and masses of bird life.

They warned him between gulps and bites which other loads he should try to avoid. Sacks of talcum powder were heavy and devilish slippery to grip and keep on your shoulders and foul iodine died your skin and clothes yellow and made you feel ill. Then there were the disgusting, slimy dog and horse skins which were sent over to France to be turned into what they called chamois leather gloves.

They talked as if there was a choice but he knew they had to take what they could get. Albert began to feel guilty that all this information was being handed to him to help him get work when, with luck, he might not be coming back and was anxious to return to the subject of this particular dock. There wasn't much time left.

As quickly as he could he brought the Freddie and toothless old Enoch back towards The London Docks. Again they wanted to describe the worst jobs for example tea-blending. It seemed when merchants wanted a blend various chests of tea were turned out onto the floor of the warehouse and casual labourers mixed it together with large, flat shovels.

'It gets up your nose, in your eyes, your ears, down your neck,' said Freddie shuddering.

Enoch grinned. 'If the posh folk what drink it knew that we stand in it in our boots when we've just come out of them horrible wet toilets!'

They all roared with laughter at that thought, miming toffs drinking tea with their little fingers in the air.

Albert tried to keep his expression alert and interested aware that any minute they would be called back to work.

At last he managed to drag them onto the subject of calling foremen. Not as subtlety as he would like but it was now or never.

Their response was the same as Jerry's: some of them were quite fair, some bloody sadistic and some were in between – just did their jobs automatically like.

'Was 'e one of the sadistic ones?' he asked casually. 'That geezer what was found dead in Trafalgar Square?'

'Myers? Nah, he was all right,' said Freddie.

'Bit of a surprise when he got that job though,' put in Enoch who had been about these parts a lot longer.

'Why's that?'

He shrugged. 'Bit strange. Come from nowhere.'

'Well, from the office,' grinned Freddie. 'But,' he agreed. 'shouldn't think he knew that much about the labouring side.'

'Must know somebody, some said.'

'Know somebody!' exclaimed Freddie. 'Blimey, it's not that great a job!'

'Who would have that sort of influence then?' asked Albert.

Freddie gave him a sideways glance. Did he seem too interested? He looked away trying to hide his excitement that he might be getting somewhere. He was desperate to take something good back to Mr Best this time.

Enoch put his grizzled head to one side and sucked his gums, 'Dockmasters. Bosses. Shippers.' Although it came out like 'Dockmashters, Boshes' and 'schlippers'.

'An' shareholders,' put in Freddie. 'It was going round that one of his family might be a shareholder in something or other. But,' he made a face, 'I can't see a shareholder being related to a docker, can you?'

Albert shrugged his shoulders. 'Dunno.' He looked puzzled. 'Don't know anything about shareholders and all that.'

A great clanging of bells prevented him from hearing Freddie's next remark. The foreman was beckoning them. Freddie stood up.

Well, he had *something* to tell Inspector Best. But he wanted more. Enough to help him on his way to Scotland Yard? He pretended not to see the gesticulating man.

'One thing *I* do know,' went on Freddie. 'He did a lot of recruiting about the yard. Neither the shareholders nor the bosses would have been very happy about that.'

'Recruiting? Who for? The army?'

Both men laughed.

'Nah!' Freddie exclaimed.

What he said next was obliterated by a bellowing shout. 'You lot! Get yourselves over here!'

Freddie glanced towards the now angry foreman who was now approaching. 'Come on!' he said. 'We got to go or we'll get paid off!'

Enoch stumbled up and Albert joined them as they walked rapidly towards the impatient work-master.

'Who for?' Albert repeated desperately, no longer attempting to hide his interest. 'Who was he recruiting *for*?'

'Oh, that lot. What do they call them? You know – the Social Democratic thingyumebobs.'

16

Albert hurried eagerly up Commercial Street. It was 7.30pm. He should just catch Florence before she went off on her rounds. He was dying to see her again. He imagined her surprise and delight. There had not been time to send a letter telling her he would come after his work at the docks.

And there she was, a tiny figure, neat in her navy blue uniform, her sweet face framed by the bonnet. Chosen, like the rest of the uniform, to eschew the evils and vanity of fashion, to be smart but not extravagant or ostentatious, the Sallies bonnet, with its large satin bow under the chin, managed nonetheless to be very becoming.

Florence was talking earnestly to a tall, handsome young swell while the flashily-dressed young woman beside him tugged at his sleeve and threw her resentful glances.

Albert waited until she had finished. The young man eventually shook his head and laughed as he walked away with the young prostitute, then looked back at Florence with a grin and a wink. Clearly he found her attractive.

As she turned and looked about her for further potential converts Albert walked over and placed himself squarely in front of her. She frowned and glanced up at him taking in the unshaven cheeks, threadbare jacket, casual neckerchief and the Great Eastern Railway cap with the cracked brim and stepped to one side to get out of his way. Another young man either about to make advances or cheeky remarks?

'It's me!' he exclaimed. 'Albert!'

She stopped and stared at him, eyes wide. 'Albert! I didn't recognise you!'

'That's good,' he grinned, 'I'm in disguise!'

He was so pleased to see her that he slipped his arm around her and bent to kiss her quite forgetting she was in uniform. She drew back instantly, shook an admonishing finger at him and smiled.

'Oh, it's lovely to see you, Albert.'

'And you too.' He gazed at her adoringly. 'Let's go back to your place so you can change and come out with me just for a little while.' He looked down at himself, aware he must look dirty and smell of sweat. At least he had been able to splash his face to remove the soot and flour and 'I could have a wash and smarten up a bit.'

And I can have a kiss and a cuddle, he thought although longing for more, excited by her proximity. Those curls escaping from her bonnet (worn, as required, far enough back to expose the hairline) were so endearingly fetching and that neat little figure in the snug jacket . . .

She shook her head. 'I'm so sorry, darling. I can't.' She pointed to the bulging satchel tucked behind a theatre sandwich board.

'Can't you leave it just this once?' he complained, disappointed and weary.

'No, I *can't*. I didn't go last night because of the fog and they *need* me!'

'So do *I*,' he exclaimed heatedly! 'I've rushed here to see you. I've been thinking about seeing you all day – and you don't care!'

'Yes I do.'

'*I* need you too,' he said again, pleadingly this time.

'Not as much as them,' she insisted. 'Some of them are starving. I thought you'd understand. It's my duty!'

He couldn't believe it. She was choosing them before him!

She took his arm and looked up at him pleadingly. 'Come with me, then I'll get them done more quickly.' She smiled and raised her eyebrows questioningly at the same time, opening up those china blue eyes.

He sighed. He was putty.

'On the way you can tell me what you've been doing in those strange clothes – and *I* will show you something which will make you realise that I care just as much as you!'

'Not possible.' He mouthed her a kiss and they set off. Neither noticed the frustrated and angry man who watched from the shadows of the boot and shoe factory doorway on the corner of White Lion Street.

As she hurried across the street towards Peabody Buildings Florence glanced back at Albert surprised to find that he was lagging behind her.

He had difficulty in moving his legs at all having spent most of the long day doing what he had imagined only inmates in Her Majesties prisons did: working a treadmill.

This one had been situated in the gigantic tobacco warehouse where the leaves were weighed, trimmed and packed. The two-man treadmill provided the energy for the hoist which moved the bales about, the pungent smell of tobacco drifting up to them in ever stronger waves as they lifted it. There were a couple of hydraulic cranes on the dockside but most of the hoists and cranes were operated by human sweat which was so much cheaper.

Long after he had finally stepped onto firm ground Albert's thighs were still quivering. Heaven knows how they would have felt if he hadn't been fit, strong and accustomed to a lot of walking. Now his legs felt stiff and almost unwilling to move. God knows how they would feel in the morning.

He had to smile when he thought how keen he had been to go out in disguise never imagining it would entail anything so hard and demeaning. He had been like a child's pet mouse on a wheel except *the mice* did it for fun and could stop when they wanted to.

On the morning trudge to the dock gates Albert had tried decide which of his fellow marchers were Poles but he found it difficult to separate them from the Russians. They didn't look any different and their all languages sounded similar to him. In any case, Poland was under the Russian yoke, even he knew that.

Among the dawn marchers he had been relieved to see Jerry, the runtish pimply young lad he had met in the holding pen on his first morning at the dock when neither of them had been selected for work.

Today, they had both been lucky. A strong east wind had blown in several sailing ships late the previous day and more than usual men were required to help unload them - including him and Jerry.

He stuck close to Jerry reckoning he stood out less with a mate and would be kept from making obvious mistakes. Jerry showed him how to mount and dismount from the treads.

'You, can do yourself a terrible mischief, if you don't do it right,' Jerry had warned. 'Terrible mischief.' He sucked at his teeth which were so overlapped that they formed a damn over which saliva occasionally spilled. 'An keep your ears open for the shout when they want you to stop.'

Stopping turned out to be an abrupt and spine-jolting experience. A piece of wood shoved between the treads serving as a brake.

But Albert was disappointed that they had been assigned to the same treadmill which meant he would have little contact with the other casuals.

Talking while working was possible but had to be shouted with the risk of being overheard so proper conversation was limited to their brief rest times after they had got their breath back. Hard as this treadmill job was, Jerry confided that it was less dangerous than the huge eight-man crane treadmills unloading the ships. 'If one man gets his foot or his leg caught its hard to get it stopped in time.'

But the big wheels were a companionable option. 'You can have a laugh on them,' Jerry confided somewhat ruefully, 'an sometimes you all sing a bit. They can unload a ton at a time, you know,' he said with some pride. 'A ton at a time.'

He had a habit of glancing at you uncertainly when he made a statement, as if afraid you might not believe him, so he repeated phrases to help convince you.

Given this lack of opportunity Albert did not wait too long after they had recovered their breath before turning to the subject of Myers and the Polish gang but covered his eagerness by pretending to be obsessed with violent crime, including the recent grisly murder of a woman in Hoxton.

'You're bloody-thirsty bugger, aren't you,' said Jerry, wiping his brow with a filthy rag.

He had heard about the rumours of a threat against Myers. 'But I 'eard it was the Tigers,' he said as tucked the rag in his belt and reached for his bait.

Albert tried to hide his surprise. 'The Bessarabian Tigers!' That was a turn-up. The Bessarabians were a South Russian gang who intimidated the East End shopkeepers and workshop owners with threats of violence if they didn't pay protection money. A threat they were only too willing to carry out with some savagery.

'Why would they be threatening a calling foreman?' he asked casually, 'Don't see the point.'

Jerry shrugged, waited until he had swallowed his first mouthful of dry bread and a bite of German sausage, then said, 'Dunno. Mebbe they want to get in 'ere to do a bit of thieving?'

Well, at least that was some news to take back to Inspector Best.

It had been cold standing in line when the day's work was done. Particularly when he was so weary and his clothes were wringing with sweat. But he had no choice. He let his mind drift from Florence, who thought him a decisive man of action, to his father who never let him make a decision for himself and if he ventured to do so, soon pointed out its flaws. If either of them could see him now! One thing he was *not* able to do was to make a decision to leave this line.

The man ahead of him shuffled forward, stiff-legged, awkward. Despite the chill Albert noticed beads of sweat on the back of the man's neck.

Another shuffle forward. Albert craned his head to look along the line to see how many men were in front of him. He was the fourth behind the man the Dock Police sergeant was now patting down. Oh, well, not long.

The sergeant's movements were practised, mechanical, his expression blank. Such a boring job searching men over and over for a bundle of Havannah cigars, a couple of oranges or a lump of gutta percha.

Albert's glance shot back to the sergeant's face. He knew him! But where from?

Had he been a neighbour when he lived at home in Bethnal Green? A friend of his father's? No, the sergeant was too young for that. Had they gone to the same school? Or, most likely and most disturbingly, had they worked together in the police?

They shuffled forward another step. Albert tried desperately to remember but his brain seized up in panic. If his cover was blown on this, his first plain clothes assignment, his prospects of becoming a detective would be in tatters.

When the sergeant turned towards the next casual worker Albert caught a full-face view. It was Collinson! P.c. Collinson! He'd been on the same shift with Albert at Stoke Newington. He must have switched to the dock company police. Better prospects and an easier life: he was a sergeant already. The owners had always wanted the Metropolitan Police to take over dock policing but they had refused to patrol private property.

Jerry was standing in the adjacent line absently gazing ahead. Albert suddenly pulled him over and took his place. He looked startled but after a warning look from Albert had the sense not to protest.

The slight disturbance was noticed, however, by the constable searching that queue and he leaned over to pinpoint the source.

Unable to home in exactly he gave the man in front of Albert a particularly thorough search making him remove his clothes. Albert, seen, perhaps, to be in league with this man who was yielding all kinds of booty, was given the same treatment: forced to remove all his clothes from the cracked railway company cap to the soil-engrained gardening boots and even the neckerchief, and his crotch felt about in a humiliating fashion.

Sergeant Collinson, becoming aware of the slowing down of the constable's queue, looked over curiously. Albert, who even while undressing had done his best to keep his face averted to the left, knew that the sergeant must have a clear enough view to recognise him. His boxing prowess had made him well known in the division.

When Collinson exclaimed loudly, 'Oh, and what's this?' Albert gave up, hoping the sergeant would realise he was on a case and that it was important no-one found out who he was. He looked around in time to see Collinson's hand stationary on the inside of the sweating man's legs. He watched, hypnotised, as the sergeant held out his hand and waited for the now shaking man to withdraw a half bottle of Jamaica rum from between his thighs.

'Move on!' the constable exclaimed. 'You're done!' He pushed Albert forward. 'Come on. Move on!'

He did so as fast as he could, relieved that Collinson was now too distracted to bother to look his way again.

As he and Florence crossed Commercial Street Albert began describing his day of endless treading, nearly being unmasked by Sergeant Collinson and tried to explain why he was at the docks. But Florence was scarcely listening. She seemed more eager to show him these Peabody Buildings and he had seen plenty of them.

'I know they are a bit bleak from the outside,' she was saying, 'but inside they are clean and roomy and,' she paused for effect, 'quite a few policemen live there with their families.'

He looked at her uncomprehendingly.

'The new police station is just up there.' She pointed to the next block North and smiled, pleased with herself.

'I know,' said Albert, frowning.

'The other people who live here are mostly skilled workers,' she went on excitedly – and decent people – I've met some of them,' she exaggerated.

Getting no response she continued uncertainly, 'And Spitalfield Market is just there,' she pointed a block south.

'I know,' said Albert. 'I was born near here, remember?'

'That's just it,' she exclaimed. 'You'd be coming back home!'

Albert stopped walking and stared at her, comprehension slowly dawning.

'And it's on *my* beat as well,' she concluded uncertainly. 'What could be better?'

The brim of her hat had kept him from seeing her whole face and her from seeing his expression. Now she turned expecting delight.

'You want us to *live* here!' he exclaimed unable to keep the horror from his voice.

'Yes, yes,' she finished weakly. 'I mean, it's ideal for both of us. I might find some better model dwellings, of course, there are lots of new ones. I'm looking at them all – well not the bad ones of course . . .'

'No!' he exclaimed. 'I don't want to live here. I want to live in Westminster like I am now - near Scotland Yard. I want to be a detective!'

She stared at him, astonished. 'You can be a local detective. You told me.'

He said nothing. Just shook his head disbelievingly.

'I thought you'd be so pleased,' she whispered, tears starting into her eyes.

'You're always saying I don't want to get married as much as you and because of my work . . .' She was crying now.

'Oh, Lord,' he said.

'He's not going to help you!' she shouted as she marched off.

17

'Mr Myers was happy in his personal life?' Best asked, beginning with the questions he deemed less likely to agitate the leader of the Social and Democratic Federation. Nonetheless, Hyndman affected surprise.

'You're not suggesting that his death might be due to jealousy over a mistress or some such thing?'

Best shrugged. 'Not suggesting anything, Mr Hyndman. These are just questions I have to ask.'

'Of course, of course, to eliminate the obvious, I suppose,' he answered placatingly. What a pompous man you are, thought Best.

'Well, you would be on quite the wrong track there. He and Mrs Myers were very happy together. Besides,' he permitted himself a little smile, 'He had a job you know as well as working for us.'

'He wasn't thinking of leaving the docks to work for you full time?'

'No,' he shook his head. 'His wasn't the pleasantest of jobs, I understand, but he felt it gave him access to the working men. Did a lot of recruiting down there.'

'I can see that. And he hadn't complained of any particular problems lately?'

'No. No more than usual. It's a tough place I hear.'

Best changed tack abruptly.

'Why have so many of your members left your organisation?'

Hyndman stiffened. 'I really don't see what this could possibly have to do with Andrew Myers' death.'

Best waved his hands in the air to brush away any suspicion that there was a sinister reason behind his question.

'I'm merely trying to get a fuller picture, you understand.' He smiled deprecatingly, 'I'm afraid I'm not as well informed about the SDF as I should be and I was hoping you would be so kind as to describe it to me since you are, I'm told, the kingpin.'

The formality and deference caused Hyndman to relax a little. He stroked his long beard and began to give his explanation as to why half his organisation, including William Morris and Eleanor Marx, had just upped and left.

'There was a difference of opinion about policy. That's all. Perfectly normal in political organisations such as ours.'

Best refrained from pointing out that there had never *been* any organisations such as theirs in Britain before. Socialist organisations that is. Apart from the abortive attempt by the Chartists in the hungry forties the SDF had been the first. Now there were three. The other two were the Socialist League and the Fabians like Annie Besant and her young Irish boyfriend, George Bernard Shaw, who were given to more intellectual discussions on democracy and the rights of man but did do their fair share of speechmaking.

'They, I'm talking about Mr Morris, Miss Marx, Mr Bax and others, but particularly Mr Morris, wished to concentrate on *educating* people about socialism – propaganda in other words - so that when the time came they would band together and. . .' He stopped abruptly.

Best effected not to notice. 'Act.' That was what he was going to say, 'act'. Revolution. He was talking about a revolution led by poet, playwright, craftsman and artist Mr William Morris.

'Whereas I favoured a gradual approach - stepping stones to socialism, I call it.' Hyndman hurried on. 'I thought we should get one or two of our candidates into Parliament as soon as possible.' He waved his hand at the view from the SDF office window in which were framed the said Houses of Parliament opposite. 'Much more practical, I thought. As you may know, Mr Burns stood in the last election. "Stepping stones to socialism" that's my motto.'

His 'gradual' approach was at odds with Champion's objections to him inflaming the masses. They all seemed to be accusing each other of revolutionary tactics.

'So, *your* view prevailed and they left?'

Hyndman sat forward. This was a matter which clearly still exercised him. 'No, as a matter of fact it didn't happen like that. It was all very strange. When the matter was voted on by the Council – Mr Morris and his cohorts actually *won*.' His lips tightened at the memory. 'By ten votes to eight.'

Best frowned in puzzlement. 'So why did they leave?'

'It's a mystery to me, too, Mr Best,' he said in his most patrician manner. 'Something about the situation no longer being viable, not being able to carry on in such circumstances, Mr Morris said.' Hyndman had been fingering a silver paper knife on his desk and now took to turning it over and over. 'So that

was that,' he said in a rush. 'Off they went and formed the Socialist League.'
There must have been more to it than that, thought Best.
'Had there been much bad feeling? Due to the disagreement, I mean?'
Hyndman shrugged, 'Oh, only as much as strongly held opinions strongly expressed usually engender. You know how it is. People get a little heated.'
He threw the paper knife down and looked up suddenly.
'I hope you're not suggesting that our policy disagreement was a motive for the murder of our poor comrade Myers?'
Best was thinking that it just might but he shook his head. 'No.'
'Ridiculous idea,' said Hyndman dismissively as if Best himself had voiced it. Interesting that. He admonishes me for something I have not said.
'Besides, it's too long ago. More than two years now.'
But it still riles, thought Best. Having half your organisation taken from you. Time doesn't always heal. It sometimes exacerbates resentments, increases them, causes them to loom larger and more lethally.

'All this publicity,' Warren slapped a newspaper on his desk. Best had seen the headline, 'WHO KILLED SOCIALIST LEADER?' so his upside down reading skills were redundant on this occasion.
'Sensationalism. We must nip it in the bud.'
He was being optimistic there, thought Best. It's out now. It will never go back in. It wasn't like censoring dispatches from the front line in Afghanistan.
James Monro nodded. scarcely hiding his irritation at this intolerable interference with his department. His recent success in helping to uncover a Fenian plot to kill the Queen had strengthened his hand at the Home Office and he wanted to continue reporting directly to them not to this toy soldier who had taken a job that was rightfully his.
'What progress, Inspector?' Warren asked Best. 'Is there a suspect yet?'
Best shook his head. "Several possibles, sir. Nothing definite yet."
Warren seemed not to be listening as he stood up and began to pace. 'They are?'
'Well, of course, it might be political. He'd just left the SDF and he had a row with an ex-member in the square that night. Or there's his work – he was a calling foreman at the docks.' Best hesitated wondering whether he should explain what a calling foreman was.
'And?'
'He'd received threats from a group of Polish casual workers.'
That got Warren's full attention. 'Ah. Good! Good'

Anything was better than political. 'So are they in custody?'

'Haven't traced them yet but,' Best hesitated, 'threats are not unusual in that job and don't usually come to much apart from a punch on the nose.'

'Is the weapon one they'd use?'

Good question.

He shook his head. 'Er, no. The weapon is a bit strange. If it *is* the weapon. We can't be sure. It was found in the fountain the following night.'

He unwrapped the parcel he was carrying with him, pulled out the oddly-curved knife and placed it on the desk.

Warren glanced down and said bluntly , 'It's a Kirpan.'

Best gazed at him, 'Er? Sir?'

Even Monro sat up a little.

'A Kirpan. A Sikh ceremonial dagger. Not a weapon. Religious significance. Traditional.'

He looked at them both and seeing incomprehension added. 'Kirpans come in all sizes. Can get them as long as three feet. No sheath found?'

Best shook his head. 'Not so far, sir.'

'Should be kept sheathed. Not supposed to be used as a weapon.'

'That's very useful sir,' said Best. 'Thank you.'

He meant it. Indian, that was interesting, very interesting. There were all sorts of Indian connections at the docks: ships, cargoes such as jute, tea, chutney, spices; Lascar seamen. There was even the Home for Asiatics who had fallen on hard times.

'Might it be used for animal sacrifice, sir?'

Warren looked startled. 'Good heavens, no!'

'It's just that blood was found along the edges and, of course, we don't know whether it's human or animal.'

Monro said nothing until they were outside and then only to vent his spleen at the man's interference. 'He should go back to fighting his Kaffir Wars. That's all the man's good for.'

Best nodded but his mind was working. Not Persian or Middle Eastern then but Indian! Might Myers have crossed one of those Lascars? Offended against their religion? That was what these things were usually about, weren't they?

Wasn't the Indian Mutiny supposed to have been sparked off because some pig and cow grease had been used on Enfield paper cartridges the ends of which had to be bitten off by the Hindu and Moslem soldiers who regarded the fat as unclean?

A good possibility then, that a British docker might as easily offend, perhaps in some unknowing way that made an Indian use a ceremonial dagger against him - symbolically perhaps?

Or maybe the dagger had been found by someone else at the docks among the imported goods. A Pole, perhaps? Ah, now they were getting somewhere.

There was another connection lurking somewhere at the back of Best's tired mind but at present it refused to present itself for inspection.

18

'Well, I can't see that someone would stab a man just because they disagreed with their policies,' said Best. 'They're all socialists after all.'

Helen laughed. '*You* have never been to a meeting of the Ladies Discussion Society when they are talking about the best way to press for women's suffrage. The knives come out there, I can tell you!' She handed him another of her paintbrushes to rinse and said, 'Anyway, aren't you always telling me how irrational people can be?'

'Yes, but Champion doesn't seem to be the sort of man who would carry one of these daggers and stick it into an old colleague. He's too controlled. Too public school.'

Helen looked at him wryly. 'In that case he'd probably get someone else to do it for him!' She paused and looked at him quizzically. 'Didn't you say Champion served in India?'

'Afghanistan.'

'Near enough.'

Best shook his head. 'It's a Muslim country. Warren says it's a Sikh ceremonial dagger.' He patted the brushes with a cloth then gave them a brisk shaking before arranging them in a jar to dry off completely.

'Yes, but India's only next door! It's not beyond the realms of possibility that he acquired the knife out there as a curio.'

'I suppose so.'

The thought which had been evading him suddenly slotted into place at the front of his mind.

'Mrs Myers!'

'Pardon?' Helen beetled her brows. Then it dawned. 'Oh, you think she might have Indian blood?' She picked up the jar of brushes and carried them to the shelf extended around the wall of her studio. 'The smouldering Mrs Myers. Not a gypsy after all. It's possible. But I haven't seen her so couldn't comment.'

'And *that's* something else,' said Best as another memory slotted into place, 'the inkstand.'

'The inkstand.' She smiled and tucked his arm into hers as they left the studio and went into the parlour. 'I'm lost.' She sat down on the sofa and patted the seat beside her. He sat down and took her hand.

No-one could call Helen a beauty. She was small and slight with grey eyes, pale brown hair and a quiet demeanour which belied her strong character.

It had been this contrast and the fact that she had not pandered to his male vanity and good looks and lacked any female coquetry that had first surprised him then allowed her to infiltrate his heart without him noticing it was happening.

The contrast between them surprised other people and caused her great amusement: the dull English mouse, as she called herself, and the handsome, exotic foreigner.

'What inkstand?' she repeated.

'The one on her desk. It was like one of those alabaster inkstands we saw being made by native craftsmen at the Colonial and India Exhibition. The ones with all those intertwining flowers. Remember?'

'Oh yes, vaguely.' She frowned, 'So?'

'Well, if she *is* part Indian . . .'

Helen laughed. 'Dearest, if I remember rightly, you rather liked them yourself and would have bought one if they hadn't been so expensive. And you're scarcely Asian. Foreign and dago-like maybe. And very handsome.' She kissed his cheek. 'But scarcely Sikh or Hindu.'

Sometimes he wished she wasn't so quite bright and outspoken but he did treasure the fact that he could talk to her about his cases particularly now that Sergeant Smith was engaged elsewhere. All his other colleagues were busy too and he rarely even had the chance to discuss his thoughts and progress on a case with his Chief Superintendent, Dolly Williamson.

Being from another world and, of course, being female, Helen sometimes brought a different point of view to bear. Focussed in on something he had missed. And he appreciated, most of the time, that she said what she really thought. Hadn't she done so when they had first met?

He could still see her reacting crisply to his impatient entry into the interview room at Scotland Yard when she came to demand action about her missing sister, Matilda. It had been the search for Matilda that had brought them together; the widower and the spinster painter.

'Still,' he said stubbornly. 'The inkstand *could* be pertinent.'

'Hmm. It could. Could it also,' she said, teasingly poking him in the ribs, 'be a sign of desperation?'

'I'm not as desperate as Warren. He's determined its not going to be political. He'd rather it be something personal – a crime of passion - or that gang of Poles at the docks.'

'You're following that up?'

'You sound like Williamson. Of course I am. Or at least Albert has been down at the docks but all he has come up with so far is another complication – Bessarabians!'

'Yeh, Mrs Myers, I heard there's a touch of the tarbrush about her,' agreed ex-Pc Alec Burns.

'Indian?' asked Best.

'Mebbe.' He shook his head. 'Dunno exactly.'

What he did know exactly was how much of the SDF felt about Hyndman: that he was an autocratic bastard.

'But your brother stays on? I wouldn't think he would be easily cowed.'

Indeed, John Burns, who was one of labour's aristocracy in that he had a trade as an engineer like his father, gave every appearance of being confident and strong-willed.

Best had heard him speak several times and had been impressed. A powerful, magnetic figure standing legs akimbo, hands thrust deep into the pockets of his blue reefer suit and his bowler hat pushed onto the back of his head. When he began his stentorian voice would emerge at full blast then, once due attention from the crowd had been gained, he would modify it and carry on in more persuasive tones. No doubt a clever man and certainly not one short of ego.

Alec Burns grinned. 'He has his reasons.' He hesitated, then looking uncomfortable, warned. 'I won't be disloyal to my brother.'

'I wouldn't ask you to be,' said Best. 'I just want to get a clearer picture of the set up.'

Alec Burns shrugged, splayed out his hands palms upward and said seriously. 'It's just that he agrees with the SDF policy more than that of the Socialist League which he thinks is fid-fadding around with all this educating the proletariat first. He thinks making a stir and getting a man elected is the only way.'

He shrugged. 'And I think he's grateful to Hyndman for getting the first socialist party going and supporting it financially.'

'How about Myers?'

Alec Burns shrugged. 'Keen member. Had had a hard life. Parents died of T.B. Brought up in an orphanage. Felt the SDF was doing something for the likes of him. I expect that's why he attacked Champion that night. Felt it was all right for the likes of him to jump ship – pick up a cause and then drop it.'

'But he didn't jump ship, did he? He was expelled.'

'Mebbe. But Myers wouldn't see it that way. Might think he was a traitor for undermining Hyndman accusing him of encouraging violent revolution.'

Oh, did he now?

Alec grinned, flexed his impressive muscles and laughed. 'They're all a bit sensitive, you know!'

'Prima donnas?'

He nodded. So the Ladies Discussion Society were not alone in their tantrums.

'They should work it off like I do!' He held up his fists in pugilistic stance. Alec Burns was a successful amateur boxer, though Albert reckoned he could now beat his teacher.

As Best thanked Alec for his help he began asking after his old colleagues and what was going on in the force now. Best sensed a great feeling of regret at no longer being part of it. He knew it was the camaraderie most policemen missed when they retired. Alec Burns had been cut off from that a great deal earlier.

'Two shillings, that's all it was,' Albert had told him. 'That's what did him. A two shilling tip.'

But, not surprisingly, the force had seen it as a bribe from someone he should have reported for obstruction and promptly sacked him.

'Let me know if you think of anything else.'

Alec nodded.

'Tell you what I do think,' he said suddenly. 'I think there's worse to come. Be careful and warn Albert to watch his back down in those docks.'

19

'Had he received any threats?' asked Best.

'Of course.' Mrs Myers held out her be-ringed hands in a gesture indicating that such things were inevitable.

Best knew she was right. The docks could be dangerous places for those in authority. Feelings ran high over supposed favouritism and unjust dismissals. Even the policemen were not safe. Their vigilance when searching the men for stolen goods and their reporting of men caught smoking - for which the penalty was instant dismissal - did not make them popular.

In recent years two policemen had died there mysteriously. One had been found drowned on the opposite side of the dock to where he should have been on his beat and another from strychnine poison given him, he managed to convey before dying, by a stranger.

But not all threats issued in the heat of the moment were followed through. Either because they were not meant seriously or the person making them lacked the means to do so.

'Were there any specific threats which appeared to be serious. From a gang say or . . .'

She sighed. 'None that he told me about. But then he didn't like to worry me.'

She bit her lower lip. An uncharacteristic gesture, Best felt, but maybe one that indicated she was not quite as sophisticated as she like to appear. There was something mysterious about this lady.

'Believe me,' she went on, 'I have been wracking my brains to think who could have done this terrible thing.'

She certainly looked sadder, more tired and slightly less immaculate than on their first meeting shortly after her husband's death. It was as if the loss was only just striking home. A not unusual reaction he reminded himself.

Numbness greeted the initial shock. Distractions came with the rallying around of friends and relatives and the necessity of arranging the funeral. Only later, when the frantic activity ceased and the attention waned, came the gradual realisation that you were now alone. It had happened like that to his mother when his father died. He kept telling her that she was not alone. She had her children. But she said he did not understand; there was no substitute for a permanent loving companion. He had learned that himself when his first wife died.

He was glad he had come back to see this handsome woman, not only because he wanted more information but it gave him a chance to review his opinions about a lady he had perhaps been too quick to see as uncaring.

Even her skin was less glowing than before and her dark hair, still coiled in a wide plait around her head appeared less lustrous. It was even slightly lop-sided as though such details no longer mattered to her.

He ploughed on, trying to stir up her memories. 'He didn't mention anything about 'a gang of Poles'? Or Bessarabians?'

Her brows knitted in surprise and she shook her head.

'Or Indians?' he added, thinking it might be a subtle way of getting her to reveal her background.

But she looked even more perplexed. 'Indians?' She repeated. 'Are you referring to those of the Asian variety, Mr Best, or the American?'

'Asian.' He hesitated. 'You see, it's possible that the knife used was a Sikh ceremonial dagger.'

He had meant to shake her composure a little and he succeeded. She blanched and shuddered. Then she sat up straight and gathered herself, thought carefully for a moment or two, then shook her head. 'It means nothing to me.'

A strange way to put it, thought Best.

'Of course,' she added quickly, 'he mentioned all the foreign sailors he had to deal with and described them to me quite picturesquely.' She smiled. 'The swarthy Lascars, those strapping Americans, the little Malaysians and so forth as well as the dockers: Germans, Poles, Italians, Russians, Irishmen – such a mixture.'

She smiled faintly, indulgently, 'He was quite proud of the smatterings of their languages he managed to pick up. Many of the dockworkers spoke Yiddish, of course and he was familiar with that having been brought up in Whitechapel.'

Her glance strayed to a photograph which lay on top of a tooled, leather-bound album, its brass clasp undone. She must have been looking at it just before he had been shown in.

This time Best had refused the offer of refreshment but as his list of questions began to peter out, he wished he had accepted. Eating and sipping and all the paraphernalia of pouring and handing over would have helped fill in the gaps while he thought about what to ask her next. Something that would not seem too crude and offensive to a newly-widowed woman.

What he wanted to do was ask her what her own background was. Where are you from Mrs Myers? Why do you seem middle class and respectable and educated but not exactly. Slightly out of place? Like an imposter?

Instead, he fell back on platitudes commenting that it must be hard for her being widowed the second time and hoping that she had plenty of supportive friends and relatives.

He soon realised that it was not a clever move. Her reaction was to become more formal while she, too, fell back on platitudes: people were so kind, she only had to ask, the SDF had promised total support ...

'Is that a photograph of Mr Myers,' Best cut in suddenly. 'May I see it?'

She flinched, her hand reaching towards it protectively.

'It would be very helpful to me. The more idea I have of the man. I mean ...'

She smiled, 'Of course,' and handed it over.

It was a typical three-quarter-length portrait. Andrew Myers stood rigidly upright and dignified, his right hand resting on the top of an immensely heavy, elaborately carved dark wood chair of the type which only seemed to exist in photographic studios. His expression was a mixture of casual confidence and embarrassment.

'He hated having his photograph taken,' put in his widow unnecessarily. 'But the SDF wanted a new one. They thought they helped the workers to become more familiar with members'.

Someone had certainly become too familiar, thought Best.

The clothes he was wearing to have his photograph taken appeared to be the same as those in which his body was found lying at the foot of Nelson's column - neither were particularly fashionable nor expensive. The apparel of a well-paid artisan. Involuntarily, Best glanced again around the room taking in the heavy damask and velvet curtains, walls lined with gilt-framed pictures and mirrors and side tables laden with costly ornaments including the Indian alabaster inkstand. Clearly the man could have afforded bespoke suits and silk top hats like his SDF leader.

Mrs Myers smiled ruefully. 'He refused to wear 'the dandified garb of the bosses.' She blushed. 'Although he put it more strongly than that! Said fancy clothes would separate him from those he cared about – the workers.'

It seemed this was a complex man. Both Hyndman and Champion wore the dandified garb of the bosses. They had been called The Top-hat Socialists. How did Myers feel about that? He could see how having modestly-garbed lieutenants suited Hyndman. It made him appear as democratic as the title of his organisation suggested when in reality he was autocratic.

But how could Myers bear being employed as a caller-on with all the distress *that* entailed for working men? To watch them struggling, fighting, even crying for the sake of a day's work. Of course there were some who claimed that employed skilled men – the aristocrats of the working class – did not regard the casuals as the real unemployed anyway but as the wastrel unemployables.

It was as though she had read his mind.

'He hated his job,' she said.

Ah. This was promising. *Decide whether to leave,* he had written in his diary under the date of his death.

'He didn't think of leaving and working full time for the SDF?'

She shook her head firmly. 'He felt at least he brought fairness to it while others had their favourites and some took bribes.'

It was possible, of course, that he had not shared his thoughts about leaving his job – or maybe the SDF – with his wife.

Had Myers perhaps told her he might be leaving her and was going to decide that day whether to or not?

Should he ask her about the bangle found in her husband's pocket? It certainly didn't look like the sort of thing she would wear. Too girlish and lightweight.

There could be a simple explanation which would eliminate this puzzling clue. But if she *was* implicated in his death it could put her on her guard. She certainly looked bereft. But wouldn't she also be grieving if she found she had lost her husband before his death? She might have acted in anger, paying someone to kill him, but still feel the grief and injury to her pride. Better leave the bangle question until later.

'How did he come to be doing that job? Best asked in what he hoped was an innocent manner not even hinting at the suggestion that she may have bought his way into the job as a docks' shareholder.

She looked at him equally innocently. 'Oh, it was a natural progression, I think. He'd worked at various jobs there, you know.'

She turned her attention to the photograph album and, without being asked, opened it and adjusted it so that he could see the contents as she described them.

*   *   *

'He looked a lot more relaxed in their wedding pictures,' said Best. 'In fact, he looked pleased and proud. Like the cat that had got the cream.'

'Not surprising, judging by your descriptions of the lady.' Helen removed her paint-stained smock, hung it up and kissed him warmly. 'So what did the wedding party look like? Any ladies in saris?'

Best shook his head. 'They were mostly his relatives but she did point out her brother and sister.' He smiled at the recollection. 'They looked like startled rabbits. Uncomfortable in their clothes and the situation.'

'And physically?'

'Well, both were middle-aged of course. He was quite a handsome fellow with dark, curly hair and nice straight features. She was dark as well but plainer and rather squat. Nothing like her sister, the bride.'

'How very unfair.'

Helen stood back, perused her day's work – a pastel portrait of Lucy Jane now five and three-quarters - shrugged then returned her attention to Best.

'One good thing though,' he said. 'There was a card in the album announcing their nuptials so I was able to get her name and previous address without having to ask her.'

'Clever you. And?'

'It was Hearn. Adeline Hearn.'

'Gypsy family name,' said Helen smugly.

'Not exclusively,' he retorted.

'No, of course not. They adopt English names when dealing with us gentiles but use quite different ones among themselves.'

'I *know that*. I've had plenty of problems finding suspects among the tribes of Stanleys, Lees's, Bosvils, Deightons and yes, even Hearns. Makes them harder to track down I can tell you.' He paused and made a face at her. 'But that still doesn't mean that *every* Stanley or Hearn is a gypsy.'

She was unmoved and made a face back.

'So what address did the card give?'

He winced, anticipating her reaction. 'Latimer Road.'

She grinned triumphantly. 'There you *are* then.'

'No, I'm *not*,' he laughed. 'Not *necessarily*.'

'Of course you are. It all adds up. Dark, smouldering, something a little strange and mysterious about her but not exactly foreign, the name and, she finished with a flourish, 'the place.'

'There *are* other people living in Notting Dale.'

'Ah, but not mysterious exotic people. Let's face it. Apart from Wandsworth in the winter and give or take a Gypsy Hill or Corner here and there, Notting Dale is *the* place for gypsies.'

'Maybe, but don't forget they cleared a lot of them away after that scarlet fever outbreak and they're building houses now on so much of that waste land they camp on. It's becoming quite a respectable area.'

'My point exactly.'

'Just a minute! *You* said .. '

The studio door burst open as little Lucy Jane rushed in, hurtled towards him and threw herself at his legs. He picked her up and hugged her.

'Besides,' he said over Lucy's head after he had duly admired her pretty new bead bracelet, 'I can't see Adeline Myers keeping pigs and living in a primitive caravan surrounded by dozens of wild children.'

'As I said, *exactly.*'

The woman could be irritating at times.

'*She* would be among those who married out, maybe to money, stopped travelling, bought one of those new houses but kept the caravan in the garden in case they changed their minds.'

He shrugged and put Lucy down.

She was probably right. He should have realised that. She knew much more about gypsies that he did.

These days, he thought, people either idealised the gypsies as exotic free spirits, especially readers carried away by the George Borrow's romantic tales of Romany life, or saw them as lazy, dirty and dishonest vagabonds.

Best was very tolerant of other races but he had to admit that most of the gypsies he had had dealings with *were* drunken, lawless and often violent. But then that was where his work took him, he thought, trying to be fair, among the lawless.

'But,' he said pulling a copy of *The Infant's Magazine* from his pocket and handing it to an excited Lucy, 'gipsies don't get married.'

'Aha!' cried Helen triumphantly. 'That's where you're wrong. Some of them *are* getting married now. A few even marrying local people *and* sending their children to school.'

'They only do that to please the preachers who give them soup and help with their problems,' he said cynically as he sat down, pulled Lucy onto his lap and opened the magazine she had thrust into his hands.

'Mrs Myers is a gypsy – or an ex-gypsy,' said Helen, getting the last word in. 'You'll see.'

20

'You'd have thought she would have known I wouldn't want to do *that*,' complained Albert.

'Had you told her?' asked Best as he shivered and banged his arms and chest for warmth. The sudden sharpness of winter in the air had caught him unawares. The day had started out deceptively sunny and bright making an overcoat seem unnecessary. It wasn't winter yet, he had told himself, but it felt like it now. All this standing about allowed the chill creep into your bones. He must be getting old!

Albert shrugged and repeated stubbornly, 'You'd think she would have known.'

Obviously Albert's habit of sharing his thoughts did not extend to his future bride. Why was that? Because he wanted to appear manly and confident?

Best could not imagine not sharing his feelings with Helen even though he wasn't always happy with her responses.

'Did *you* know that Florence wanted to stay down in the East End?' he said, feeling like a parent trying to placate warring children.

Albert felt under his helmet strap and worried the sore spot where it chaffed his fair skin.

'No.' He shrugged eventually. 'But that's different, innit? You got to go where the man's work is, haven't you? I'm the one with the proper job, aren't I?'

He stared morosely out over the square which was quieter now than yesterday when milling crowds had gathered in preparation for their march to St James's Palace 'to see the Queen's Jubilee presents'.

'Dunno how we're going to live on my wage anyway,' he muttered quietly. 'It's a pittance. A pittance for working these terrible hours and suffering all this aggravation.'

He did, indeed, look worn out. Small wonder so many police officers died from pneumonia and tuberculosis. All that exposure when exhausted.

Pittance, that was a new word in Albert's vocabulary.

'What we want is one of them unions. Mebbe *we* should start standing up making speeches and agitating.'

Ah, that was where he got it from. Did the Commissioner and the Home Office realise that some of the political messages in the speeches might be getting through to those most exposed to them: the policemen obliged to keep watch.

Maybe, if they were, they might not have been so quick to hand over to the police orphanage the money the public had subscribed to the police in recognition of all the extra work they were doing. The Orphanage was a worthy cause but . . .

'They don't care about us,' Albert complained. 'Look at yesterday while we was waiting around for that march to start. We'd had starved or died of thirst if it weren't for the vicar over there.' He waved his arm towards the church of St Martins-in-the-Field.

Noticing how tired and hungry the policemen looked the vicar and his churchwardens had produced tea, coffee, bread and butter and sandwiches for them. The act had touched them deeply, particularly because it was offered in a venue in which they were constantly being harangued as brutal thugs.

In the end, yesterday's proposed march to see the Queen's presents had been postponed. The reason, it was suspected, was the heavy police presence marshalled to accompany the marchers and the number of extra guards posted around St James's Palace. Not to mention the threat of rain.

Whatever the cause, the authorities had been much relieved by the cancellation having doubted that it was a gesture of patriotism but more likely an opportunity to point up the difference between her condition and theirs. It had not been very difficult to discern their real aims given that the request to view the presents on exhibition had been made on behalf of 'Her Majesty's unemployed slaves'.

Today, the organisers had been teasing the police about the possible destination of today's march. Should it be St Paul's Cathedral or Westminster Abbey they suggested mischievously. Some of the more rowdy marchers had caused a great deal of disruption during an Abbey service last Sunday: swearing, shouting, climbing up and even urinating on the statues and the floor of the church.

As usual police, mounted and on foot, were drawn up on both sides of the Square ready to quell trouble or march alongside the crowd wherever they might choose to wander this time.

In the event, the procession had marched through the West End streets carrying two large red flags and accompanied by the band of the Lambeth branch of the SDF playing the *Marseillaise* as well as Albert and a number of his colleagues.

Albert had been glad of the chance to stretch his legs even though the marching aggravated his skinned heel. His worn-in but soaked boots were drying out on the radiator in the section house so he was wearing a new pair made of leather as hard as concrete. Warren was right. Their boots were rubbish.

Back in the Square now and standing still at least offered relief to the sore heel and listening to the speeches helped alleviate the boredom. They had been instructed to watch out for seditious and violent language from the speakers. Hard to tell which was the first and the second, in Albert's opinion, depended on the way things were said.

A 'Comrade Calvert' was advocating the nationalisation of the land, railways, machinery and all means of transit and finished by repeating the Socialist chant: 'They are few. We are many. You must win and they must lose!'

Maybe they are right. We are fools to put up with all this, Albert thought. The fact that his legs had begun to ache through standing rooted to the spot for so long and now his right toes were feeling scraped and raw added to his feeling of being, what his mother called, 'badly done to'.

An ex-soldier up on the platform began berating Warren for using the same brutal measures against civilians such as them as he had against his unfortunate soldiers.

Yeh, that's me, he thought. Brutal. One of Warren's Wolves. The thing was, if any violence did occur now, would he be able to get his legs to move in time to deal with it?

To take his mind of boots and brutality he began to mull over the facts of 'their case'. The bangle, for example. Best did not think it could be a present for Mrs Myers because it was not the kind of thing she would wear and the man had no daughter or granddaughter.

There was a suspicion that it might have been a present for a mistress. Well, Albert had heard Myers giving speeches and knew he had a job which kept him working hard all day. Then there was all this SDF business. When would the man have the time for Mrs Myers, never mind a mistress? In any case it was a young woman's bangle and somehow he just couldn't see this middle-aged dock worker cavorting with some young girl.

There had to be a simpler explanation. He was looking after it for another relative or colleague? He had stolen it? Or – or. . . That was it! That *must* be it! Why hadn't they thought about it before? Wait till he told Best! No, he wouldn't tell him, he would follow it up himself *then* tell him. Show him he could act on his own initiative.

Around five o'clock the sky darkened rapidly and an ominous rumbling noise passed across the heavens. A spatter on raindrops began bouncing off Albert's helmet and onto his cheeks. Then came the deluge. Rain and hail pounded and bounced off the flagstones soaking into Albert's uniform and seeping into the space between his socks and his concrete boots.

The speakers and the crowd ran for the cover of Morley's Hotel to the east and the Union Club and the Royal College of Physician's to the West though they were clearly not going to be welcome at either. The younger ones with longer legs sprinted for the shelter of the National Gallery and St Martin's-in-the-Field's Church porticos to the north.

All right for them, Albert thought.

Thus, he was depressed again when Best saw him that evening and not only because he had fallen out with his beloved Florence.

At least the air had that crystal clarity which follows heavy rain. The atmosphere of smoky, foggy London had been given the washing it desperately needed.

At first, as dusk began to fall, only a few people hung about in the square but soon small, vociferous groups began to gather, occasionally firing angry glances at the police.

'It's them rioters over in America what killed the policemen,' said Albert who was tuned in to everything that went on. 'They're going to hang them soon.'

It was eighteen months since the Haymarket bomb had exploded so devastatingly and fifteen months since five of the accused had been sentenced to death. To the wonder of the British Press the time since then had been taken up with attempts to get the verdict set aside by superior courts, through various appeals and via worldwide petitions.

In Britain, which had no court of appeal, the various socialist and anarchist groups had joined forces to hold a meeting to protest against this 'judicial murder'.

Agitating these agitators even more were the allegations that most of the Haymarket police deaths had not been caused by the bomb but by their own bullets when they opened fire on the crowd and that they had killed more protestors than deaths suffered by themselves. Worse, some of the accused had not even been in the square at the time but had been picked up in a sweep of trouble makers.

The fate of those awaiting execution was now in the hands of the State Governor.

'There'll be trouble *here* if they do hang 'em – even though its nowt to do with us,' said Albert. 'And, of course the Irish are getting all heated about that O'Brien business.'

William O'Brien M.P. had been taken into custody for helping organise a rent strike and three of the tenants had been shot dead while demonstrating against his arrest. This incident now had one of those names that become rallying which light touch paper: the Michelstown Massacre.

'Remember Michelstown!' cried Irish speakers in the square.

Albert and Best were morosely contemplating these escalating problems when a violent scuffle broke out in the midst of one of the small groups milling about. An angry, bald-headed little man, his spectacles askew, was shouting and trying to punch one of the speakers. 'You're ruining our trade!' he yelled. 'These layabouts are driving me out of business! I'll be the one out of work! And they don't want any!'

Albert sighed. 'There's trouble brewing. Real trouble', he pronounced. 'And we'll be right in the middle of it.'

21

It was a wonder to Best how such a dismal and forlorn place was allowed to exist so close to the handsome town mansions of Holland Park. It was even quite near to genteel Bayswater and no great distance from Mayfair and London's fashionable West End.

Another source of wonder was the rapid rate at which the area was being eaten up by new housing developments that were spreading ever further North and West swallowing up the remaining farms of Notting Hill and the brickfields of Shepherds Bush.

When first laid out in the 1840s Latimer Road cut North/South through waste land and brickfields parallel with and quite close to the South Western Railway line and stood curiously isolated from any other habitation.

From then on, its development occurred in a patchwork fashion. Newly-built houses sat right next to empty plots and patches of wasteland. Now most of the plots and the waste land alongside Latimer Road was filled. Gypsies had wintered in Notting Dale for many years, some families even putting the railway arches to good use as shelter. Now they squatted on land partially torn up for brick clay, partially cleared in preparation for more building and partially occupied by some just-completed, newly-occupied houses.

Even as Best arrived more travellers were coming in after spending the summer and autumn in the countryside helping farmers bring in their crops.

Once they found a space on this chaotic, overcrowded stretch of land, they would unhitch their caravans or unload their curved bender tent frames from their carts, set them up, duly drape them with coverings, furnish them with their scant belongings and release dirty-faced children, cats, dogs and chickens onto the site.

Best was thankful that the pigs were gone. The smell of them had been atrocious and the battle by the authorities to get rid of them for sanitary reasons had been long and hard.

A young woman with a baby strapped to her back was pegging out washing on a line stretching from a decrepit medium-sized caravan to the wall of a nearby shack. Helen used to come home from sketching down at Notting Dale unhappy about the lives of the gypsy women.

'They're virtually slaves!' she would exclaim. 'All the responsibilities are on their shoulders!'

And it certainly sometimes looked like that. He had seen a gypsy woman with one child on her back, another in one arm and a basket of clothes pegs and carved wooden toys on the other.

But he had also seen gypsy men working - sharpening knives in the street or sitting at the kerbside weaving new chair bottoms for a householder. It had to be admitted however that some of the men were ferocious drinkers and that was the cause of much suffering among the women.

He headed for one of the well-kept, larger traditional caravans set apart from the others and with plenty of space around it. Clearly Jake Bosvil, or to give him his gypsy name, Chumo-mescro, was the current king of the place, the cock of the green, or *rex loci*.

He recognised the man's caravan from the description given him by Constable James, the local constable: painted deep red with entwined roses around the door.

The chimney was puffing blue-grey smoke out into the already grey sky of the dreary, early November day. Obviously someone was at home.

Two little girls of about Lucy's age sat on the steps. The pair were cleaner, better dressed and clearly better fed than most of the other children on the site. They were holding up their rag dolls, shaking them and wagging their fingers at them. On seeing Best they jumped down and, chattering away, presented the dolls for his inspection.

He understood only half of what they were saying but he now had experience of the way the minds of little girls' worked and realised that the dolls must have been naughty, very naughty. He duly frowned and shook his head and finger at them which made the little girls collapse into giggles. Children were all the same, he thought, although doubtless most of them on this site would soon be put to earning their keep.

'Hello, what's to do?'

A powerful-looking man of about forty years had appeared at the door. He was quite tall, just under Best's height of five foot eleven inches. His head, supported by a short, thick neck, had the broad, jowly look of a bull mastiff. But it was the chest and arms which took the eye. The chest was very broad and heavily muscled and the arms were long and strong, the biceps straining against his rolled-up shirt sleeves. Huge, bony hands completed the powerful picture. This must be Jake Bosvil.

Best disengaged himself from the giggling little girls and stepped forward, explained who he was and what he wanted. Just a little information about the community but nothing which was likely to bring any trouble on them.

'Constable James said you might be able to help me,' he concluded.

Bosvel nodded and beckoned him inside. It seemed that Constable James's name was a password into this closed world.

Hitherto the only gypsy caravans Best had been inside were poorly furnished and quite squalid. Not a description he would apply to Bosvil's splendid abode with its rich carpet, shining brass ornaments and padded armchairs.

According to Constable James, Jake Bosvil was a wealthy travelling horse dealer who owned a house but still used the caravan to get about on business. His father had sent him to school and he had done quite well for himself but now felt stranded halfway between two worlds. To some extent, James claimed, Bosvil had begun to despise his fellow gypsies for their ignorance and dishonesty while finding slightly ludicrous the people who were bound by the pretensions and petty snobberies of static living.

'It'll be about Myers, is it?' he said when they had settled down into the high-backed chairs.

Best nodded. Helen had been right.

'Did you know him?'

He shook his head. 'No, but I knew Adeline. Went to school with her. Well, not exactly *with* her. She was older than me. Two classes above.' He laughed showing strong, white, chipped teeth. 'Seemed a big difference then – a couple of years. But we stuck together us gypsy children.' He shrugged. 'Self defence.'

'The other children?'

Bosvil grinned and spread those large, brown hands. 'They didn't like us. Neither our own kind nor the others.'

Did he mean the other poor children? Or the non-Romany gypsy children. Helen had warned him that gypsies didn't see themselves as all being members of one tribe. Some of them hated each other.

'Did you know her first husband?'

'Old Joe Ratzie-mescro?' He nodded then added, 'Joseph Hearn to you.'

'A wealthy man?'

'He certainly was. Worked hard for it though. First off with scrap metal then horse-dealing like me.'

'There's money in that?'

He looked around him pointedly. 'Oh, yes. But you've got to be honest to do well at it. Not do people down or ring the horses. It soon gets around if you do.' He paused then said, 'Anyway, getting back to Joseph Hearn. When he'd made his pile he looked around, saw Adeline growing up so lovely. She was only half gypsy you know,' he said in an aside. 'Her mother was a farm girl from Hertfordshire. A fair little thing. Anyway,' he reverted to the matter in hand, 'Joseph Hearn set out to win Adeline. Even bought a house and came in from the road – for a lot of the time at least.'

'Was he much older than her?'

He considered this. 'Fifteen years, I'd say.'

'He didn't have another woman?'

It was unlikely that he didn't. Although they didn't marry the gypsies formed bonds and had children early.

'Oh, I think there was someone. But I expect he took care of her. He was a decent enough man.'

'And when he died there were several suitors for Adeline?'

He smiled. 'Oh, yes!' You could call them that!'

'Any particularly ardent ones?'

He looked wary. Pursed his lips, then said. 'You're looking for suspects for Myers' murder?'

'Not necessarily. Just trying to get the full picture.'

'Hmm.'

The man was no fool.

'It was a long time ago, you know.'

'Not that long.'

'They'd have got over it. Out on the road an all ... Takes your mind off things.'

Or gives you time to brood, thought Best.

Bosvil rubbed his chin thoughtfully then said decisively, 'Well I will give you one. Never liked the man. George Deighton.'

'Where would I find him?'

'He should be coming in hereabouts any time, now all the fruit and potatoes are picked.'

'And the other one?' smiled Best.

There was a silence.

'I'll find out in the end,' said Best although he doubted he would without the help of a gypsy, their world being shut off to the likes of him. 'I'll be very discreet and, if the man is innocent, he will never even know he was a suspect. I'll find another excuse to talk to him.'

'All right. I was very fond of Adeline. Sweet on her, in fact. We all were.' He took a deep breath. 'Arthur Cooper – one of the Vardo-mescroes. He's a good man, mind. Has a woman and a young son.'

'Thank you.'

Bosvil nodded a little unhappily.

'Doing it this way is better,' Best assured him, 'rather than coming down heavy-handed on all of you and causing great disruption and ill-feeling.' He paused. 'So Myers was also from a gypsy family?'

'Oh, no!'

Best frowned. 'Well, from a settled family around here, then?'

He shook his head. 'Not that I know of.'

Best was puzzled. 'But she told me that their families had been friends for years.'

Bosvil shook his head again then stopped, raised his right forefinger and waved it saying, 'Hop-picking.'

'Ah.'

That made sense. It wasn't just the Cockneys who made the traditional autumnal hop-picking trek to the Kent. Gypsies went down there as well after a summer of picking strawberries, cherries, peas, and beans. Thrown together like that, all doing the same work, children playing together, the inevitable suspicion and reluctance was often put aside and some gypsy and East End families became lifelong friends.

'Gypsies get on fairly well with the coster families. They have a lot in common. Buying and selling and all that.'

And dodging the law, thought Best. The police had a lot of trouble with the costermongers who sometimes even ganged up on them and defied the law.

Why, thought Best, do I feel this is all becoming too complicated: dockworkers, Poles, Bessarabians, the Socialist Democratic Federation, the Socialist League and now gypsies and costermongers?

22

Best stood under the central portico of the National Gallery idly watching the crowd gathering, yet again, in the square below.

The view beyond the mob right down Whitehall as far as the splendidly Gothic towers of the Houses of Parliament in the distance was a particularly splendid on this cold but bright day.

How ironic, he thought, that gazing in the same direction from the south end of the square on the very spot from which all distances from London were measured stood the equestrian statue of King Charles I; the very man who had brought about England's only Civil War. Behind him, now, some of the speakers seemed to be trying to bring about another one.

To the left of the view was the Palace of Whitehall where the arrogant King had lost his head for his impertinence. How typical of the British that the monarchy should have later been restored and that the King's persecutors had been put to death on the very spot where his statue now stood.

It seemed that everything went around in circles. Even if these current disturbances did bring about a revolution, as so many feared, would the final result be the same, he wondered? The same privileged people reasserting control?

He was feeling uncharacteristically depressed due to an aching molar which he hadn't had time to do anything about, a cold he was sure was starting and a deep sense of foreboding. Was there no way out of this mess? The crowds kept gathering, marching, protesting, their mood becoming harsher and angrier all the time.

Of course, they weren't the only ones who were angry. The local shopkeepers and hoteliers were furious. They complained of lost trade because their customers were too fearful to come to the West End and having to close their doors and put up shutters whenever the mob gathered and went marching which seemed to be all the time now.

Their response to the 'Remember Michelstown!' cry was to shout, 'Remember South Audley Street!'

South Audley Street, being the most exclusive of the West End shopping venues attacked by the mob on Black Monday when they went smashing shop windows and looting.

The businessmen, too, were complaining that they could not move about the city to conduct their business without fear of interruption or harassment.

Everyone kept asking what the police were going to do about it.

The police themselves were also unhappy. Best could see Albert, standing, yet again, on the edge of the mob who, encouraged by the speakers, were shouting abuse at him and his colleagues.

Albert was worn out, felt unappreciated, underpaid, had small chance of a receiving a pension if he was injured on duty, a blister on his heel and was sad because he couldn't get to see his Florence to make up after their quarrel.

Like the rest of the police what he wanted was better pay, the opportunity to confer and a day off every week not just two a month. This year, they had been given the right to vote in general elections but it was not enough. They wanted to be able to talk to each other about their conditions.

Best was concerned about what Albert would do if the crowd cornered him when isolated as they had some policemen. Would he lash out in anger or would his indecisiveness and Florence's remarks about police brutality cause him to hold back - fatally?

He even felt a little sorry for Commissioner Warren, autocrat though he was. People kept criticising him and urging him to action but force rumour had it that he kept trying to get the Home Secretary to give him further powers to avert the looming disaster but was refused.

Meanwhile, he had the worry that the Fenians might seize the opportunity to plant more bombs or try to assassinate the Queen. If they did, that would break their truce and ensure the Home Rule Bill would not be passed, which in turn would ensure more disturbances. No wonder Warren was anxious that this murder case was cleared up or that another might occur.

A tall, wiry-bearded figure with the deep-set eyes was rapidly climbing the gallery steps towards Best: SDF Executive Councillor, John Burns. He wore his usual uniform of blue reefer suit, white shirt, wide black tie and a black bowler hat which he switched for a white straw in summer.

Burns was an electrical engineer, one of the skilled workers whose self-protective unions and restrictive practices had caused leading socialist, Frederick Engels, to dub them, despairingly, the labour aristocracy. Burns thus sat halfway between the wealthy Hyndman and the unprotected labouring poor although he had suffered for his SDF membership having been blacklisted from most of the larger factories following his arrest on the previous year's Black Friday.

There was no denying the man's magnetic personality. He exuded strength and vitality. It was said that if the wind was in the right direction his powerful voice could reach an audience of twenty thousand. A bit of an exaggeration, Best felt, but not a big one.

Best stepped forward and held out his hand. 'Inspector Best. Mr Hyndman is not here yet.'

Burns hesitated then took it giving Best a wry grin and a firm handshake. 'He's waiting for us inside.'

'He's an art lover?'

Burns shook his head and fell in beside Best as they entered the gallery.

'Making it his business to find out what our money's is being wasted on now, I shouldn't be surprised.'

The recent purchase of a Raphael *Madonna and Child* from the Duke of Marlborough for an astonishing £70,000 - more than three times the price ever paid for a painting – had caused quite an uproar in the socialist Press. They found the idea of £14 a square inch was just too much to swallow considering how many mouths that money could have fed.

'In truth,' admitted Burns with a cheeky grin, 'he'll probably be looking at the Dutch interiors. Says he likes the way they show ordinary people going about their business. Find them a bit gloomy myself. All those poky little rooms and grey skies.'

Best resisted pointed out that Hyndman would never have had to live in a poky little room so could afford to wax lyrical about them.

Burns directed Best up the vestibule steps grimacing as he went at Van Dyke's huge and highly flattering portrait of Charles I, magnificent in glowing armour gazing disdainfully down on them from a very large horse. 'He was only a weedy little fellow, you know,' said Burns dryly, 'and certainly never went into battle.'

He held out his right hand to direct them through the glories of the Italian galleries and on to Gallery Ten, the first of the Dutch and Flemish rooms. There they found the top-hatted figure of Hyndman gazing up at, not a cosy, domestic Dutch interior, but Lunden's copy of Rembrandt's famous, *The Night Watch*. A painting which, Best guessed, reflected Hyndman's leader-of-men aspirations.

Standing there, his pudgy hands resting on his portly stomach, a gallery guide respectfully pointing out various salient features, Hyndman looked more like a wealthy Gallery Trustee rather than the leader of a group of militant socialists.

While they waited for the guide to finish speaking Burns gave Best a sidelong glance and muttered, 'I hear you've been talking to my brother.'

Best nodded. 'Just filling in a bit of background.'

'Hmph. You could have asked us. Alec's no expert in the affairs of the SDF.'

Best shrugged. 'Sometimes those outside see more.'

Burns raised an eyebrow. 'You took advantage of his loyalty to an old friend.'

'Of course,' said Best raising an eyebrow in return, 'wouldn't you?'

Their eyes met and they both laughed.

'You know that we are trying to help improve police conditions. Even form a union?'

Best nodded. He certainly did.

Earlier in the year copies of handbill headed 'Police Grievances' had been handed to all the lower ranks out on the streets. It called on all taxpayers to attend a meeting to be held in Hyde Park to air these grievances. Hyndman and John Burns had both shown up and spoken there. A week later, questions about police hours of duty were asked in the House of Commons.

Surprisingly the men in the Commissioner's Office had not seemed unduly worried about this. They claimed that it was a case of a few discontented men being exploited by people who had no genuine concern for their welfare. Best, too, while acknowledging the need, had doubts about their motives. A police force in disarray, unwilling to act against them, would suit the agitators just fine.

Burns was watching him closely. He is about to ask me where I stand on that question, thought Best. But the guide had finished speaking and Hyndman, looked up, acknowledged them and came over, his hand held out towards Best.

'How nearer are you to a solution, officer?' he asked when the preliminaries were over and they had found a corner in the vestibule where they could sit and talk in private. His peremptory manner had been somewhat softened by the realisation that Best was not going to be intimidated.

'Not much,' Best admitted. 'Although we have tried very hard.'

He went on to list their lines of enquiry, hoping that their comments might open up another which had never occurred to him. People liked to show they were cleverer than mere policemen and sometimes gave themselves away while doing it.

'We have made extensive enquiries down at the London Dock,' he began.

Hyndman looked surprised. 'May I ask why, officer?'

'Well, the man worked there,' he replied not troubling to keep mild irritation out of his voice. 'It's an obvious starting point for one line of enquiry. All kinds of disagreements can arise among fellow workers, particularly in a job which arouses such resentments.'

John Burns nodded firmly but Hyndman looked blank. Best wondered whether he had even been down there among his unemployed, struggling to get work.

'Any result?' he asked.

'One or two possibilities. Threats made, and so on. That is hardly unusual. But,' he admitted, 'nothing concrete so far.' He paused. 'Have you any ideas about that?'

They both shook their heads but Burns said. 'It's a volatile place. I can see the dangers. But he was on the side of the workers.'

'People don't always see it that way, unfortunately.'

'But why,' said Hyndman slowly, 'would they come up to a place as public as Trafalgar Square when there must be hundreds of dark corners among the sheds and piles of cargo where the deed could be done. It doesn't make sense.'

'Murder often doesn't,' said Best then pointed out, 'of course they may have wanted to make a point by killing him right the centre of London a place where there was such unrest.'

'You know, he recruited for us down there,' said Burns suddenly. 'Discreetly of course.' He paused thoughtfully. 'But I would imagine that would upset the bosses more than the workers.'

'We did wonder about that,' Best admitted.

'But again,' said Hyndman testily, 'why would the bosses do it in such a public place?'

'Who knows,' said Best. 'A warning?'

What he did know but wasn't saying was that another knife had been found hidden away among the bushes outside the Gallery. A garbling knife such as was used to cut away damaged and extraneous leaves from the tobacco stacks in the London Dock. It might be significant. It might also be an attempt to confuse them.

But Best's present task was to placate these men to prevent them causing too much fuss in the Press against the police thus pushing another thorn into their sides.

To this end, he threw at them Bessarabians, lascar seamen, Poles, disgruntled dockers, Mrs Myers' possible suitors and jealous gypsies. Then he added interviews with Champion and investigations into Myers's private and working life into the mixture and gave it a good stir, supplying sufficient detail to give them the feeling that they were privileged insiders. He knew that everyone was fascinated by detective work, and wanted to feel as though they were in the know.

He hoped he had thoroughly confused them and given the impression that a great deal of effort was being put into the case despite the current horrendous demands on police time. Perhaps, he thought, they might even begin to feel a little guilty about the latter, particularly since they claimed they were supporting members of the force in their fight against bad conditions and long hours.

'I'm hoping you can help me,' he said suddenly throwing the ball to them.

'Us?' said a bemused Hyndman.

'Yes,' said Best briskly. 'Any enmities, petty jealousies, resentments among your ranks?'

'Oh, no,' exclaimed Hyndman. 'We're all working for the same cause and. . .'

Best gave him an old-fashioned look.

Burns had the grace to look faintly embarrassed but before Best could point to the well-known splits: Champion, Morris, Eleanor Marx and several others, he said, 'Of course. All organisations have them. We will certainly give the matter great though, Mr Best, and see if we can come up with any suggestions. But, of course, we find it very hard to think any of our members would commit murder over *policy* disagreements.'

'Naturally,' agreed Best aware that murders had been committed for much less.

'And Myers,' he enquired 'he had no plans to leave the SDF as far as you know?'

And take some of your secrets with him?

'I think you'll find,' said Hyndman getting to his feet and picking up his hat, 'that we have rid ourselves of our most dissenting comrades and are now forging ahead as one.'

They were backing away now. Passing the parcel back to the police. Any suggestion that they might be implicated in the death of one of their own would, of course, defeat their cause before it got off the ground. Best sighed with relief. Mission accomplished but his tooth still throbbed.

23

She didn't *look* disgusting, thought Albert. In fact, she looked like an ordinary little woman of about forty with a pretty face, turned up nose and wonderful voice. He envied the way she was able to put things and with such passion. He wished he could talk to Florence like that.

The crowd didn't seem to find her 'filthy and depraved' either judging by their loud cheers when she was introduced.

She soon made it plain she didn't believe what had been said about them either; that they were loafers and loungers and the scum of the earth. They were just men who wanted to work.

'Look how many loafers and loungers there are in broadcloth?' she exclaimed. 'Why should the shabby loafer be scoffed at and the others treated with respect?'

That brought more cheers.

Had she been there, Florence would also have cheered Annie Besant. She thought her a heroine for the way she stood up against sweated labour proclaiming her disgust for payment given to outdoor matchbox workers: 2 pence farthing for a gross and after buying their own string and paste.

Now Annie was suggesting work which could be offered to the unemployed such as cleaning public buildings and helping at the post office at Christmas.

'The upper classes do not like the lower classes and say "let them go back to their slums and starve". Well the lower classes do not like them so there is no love lost.'

Above all, she said, they must keep coming to Trafalgar Square despite being declared an eyesore and not being wanted there. Who knew, they might even shame the upper classes. More cheers.

The only person who didn't cheer was a wild-looking figure wearing a torn pea-jacket. He just shouted angrily. 'Look what all you trouble makers have done to me! Look!'

Public gatherings, particularly those involving a lot of shouting and cheering, tended to attract people who had lost their grip on reality. This particular person had become a familiar sight, roaming around looking agitated and shouting at the speakers. Albert knew a little about him and thought he might have reason to be a bit off his head. But as long as he didn't do anyone any harm or cause too much of a nuisance he let him be.

Listening to the speeches was no longer just a way to help Albert pass the time. He was now obliged to listen out for the use of violent or threatening language. Speakers using inflammatory language must now be pulled down from the platform and, if they refused to stop, arrested.

The Commissioner himself had been coming into the Square recently and had heard some wild threats made by the speakers. In Albert's opinion, and he was becoming a bit of an expert on the subject, these were meant solely to stir up the crowd. There was no intention of acting upon them.

Annie was clearly not going to advocate violence in fact she kept warning the crowd against it saying that it would play into the hands of those who wished them ill. So Albert could allow his attention to wander to his most pressing problem: Florence and the question of where they should live.

Now he'd had time to think about it, it warmed his heart to think of the trouble she had gone to find them somewhere. Then he felt miserable again when he thought how hurt she had been by his response. How selfish and brutish he must have seemed.

Maybe Best was right. Instead of aiming at Scotland Yard he should try to become a local detective first: perhaps in Bethnal Green.

He got the feeling that Best thought he would have a better chance of achieving that anyway, him not having any second language yet.

Best said that Scotland Yard detectives needed foreign languages because they often escorted prisoners to and from the Continent and added that that could be quite a boring task. In fact, he made it sound as though being a local detective in the East End would be much more exciting and interesting.

But then his friend, Eddie Chapman, told him that the Yard detectives had the best time and met lots of interesting and important people. Maybe Best was just trying to steer him into the job most likely to keep him and Florence together. He must ask some more friends to help him decide.

The more Albert thought about it, the more he wanted to see Florence and tell her how much he was thinking about it and apologise for what he had said. He couldn't risk losing her to some Salvation Army Captain. She meant everything to him.

Maybe he *should* have explained to her before about his ambition. But they had so little time together these days when they did meet all they could do was catch up with what had been happening to them right then. In any case, a woman wouldn't understand about police work.

When he had finally got back to his cubicle in the Section House last night he had scribbled her a letter but was worried that he because he was so tired he hadn't been unable to find the right words.

He was dragged back to the present by the shouts of the crowd who were becoming quite excitable.

Annie Besant quickly reminded them not to play into the hands of their enemies. She was, she told them, about to go and try to get some of their kind out of prison and didn't want to have to rescue any more of them. That made them laugh.

They listened with respect. When it came to prison she knew what she was talking about. She had served time herself. Not for shouting abuse or threats but for helping to publish some book about birth control.

The prosecution mouth-piece had said something about no decently-educated Englishman allowing his wife to read the book, encouraging as it did sexual intercourse without the natural result ordained by providence.

His Florence already knew about all that working with fallen women as she did. Albert wasn't sure how he felt about that. Not happy really.

Annie had told the snooty mouth-piece that desperately poor women knew everything about the natural results ordained by providence and they had had enough of them. She had been sent to prison just the same but eventually released on appeal.

It was a grey, damp and depressing day and as another speaker took over, the rain started again. The crowd began to melt away, one section moving as a body to towards The Strand. They were led by the final speaker who was dogged assiduously by the only man who hadn't cheered or laughed.

Superintendent Huntley, the man in charge that day, sensed what they were up to: forming a march. That was now also forbidden. The only procession to be allowed that day was the celebratory one in honour of the new Lord Mayor of London.

Huntley beckoned forward some of the mounted branch and foot policemen, including Albert, to accompany the Strand-bound mob.

Albert drew the collar of his cape tighter around his neck trying to keep some of the rain from trickling down his neck and soaking his tunic once again. The bottom of his trousers were already sodden.

It was farcical, he thought, as *they,* the police, marched along in the road making sure the mob kept to the pavement and so didn't form a forbidden march!

Florence could have cried as she passed the monumental Peabody Buildings in Commercial Street. She had been so pleased with herself that night and excited about their future together but her very own Warren's Wolf had soon put a stop to that!

Since then, she had thought and thought about where they could live but had given up her grand plan to visit all the new model housing in the area. There was no point.

Why, she kept wondering, hadn't he told her he didn't want to live down here? Why, come to that, she admitted to herself, hadn't she explained to him that *she* must?

As it happened, she was no longer expected to live there now after all. Not since General Booth, impressed by her work and sense of duty, had offered her charge of a rescue home for fallen women in Liverpool. This was a great honour, particularly given her age, and it was really her duty to go where she had been called. But what about her and Albert? No, this was not a solution to their problems: the reverse.

She must speak to him. But he was always on duty. So was she, much of the time, and there was no way of contacting him quickly to see whether they could snatch an hour or two at the same time.

She'd been up to Commercial Street Police Station twice and the telegraphist there had been kind enough to contact Albert's station to check on his duty roster. But she couldn't keep asking as he wasn't supposed to do it. In any case, Albert often worked well after the time he was supposed to finish. If he wasn't on duty in the square or escorting the marches he would be keeping back the crowds at one of the Jubilee events or standing guard on the Queen's Presents at St James's Palace.

She would answer his letter when she got home tonight. She had been putting it off in the hope she would be able to see him first. A letter was a poor substitute for a heart to heart meeting.

Was she or wasn't she going to go into Peabody Buildings? He'd be furious if she did. He wanted her to visit the destitute in dimly-lit backstreets and alleys. He had made a thorough inspection of her usual route and found a couple of ideal places. Dark places, waste land where nobody went. Hidden places.

He *must* get rid of her soon or his luck would run out. He could feel it. This had all gone on too long. He was desperate to get back to his usual haunts and habits without the risk of her pointing him out and calling the police.

He bunched his fists, fighting back his fury. This time, he must not act hastily. Why, he fumed yet again, did she have to come to see Jenny that night? Because she was an interfering bitch, that's why.

Jenny had been going to be such a good earner for him – once he had persuaded her.

But this bitch had got there first and done some persuading herself. Told her that it wasn't too late for her to be saved for the Lord. Well, he sniggered, the Lord had her now whether he wanted her or not. And the others besides.

So here *it* was at last, Best *thought: the declaration of war. Warren had at last persuaded the Home Secretary to agree to some action. The result was warning placards (four thousand of them) posted in the streets and published in the newspapers:

NOTICE!

MEETINGS IN TRAFALGAR SQUARE

In consequence of the disorderly scenes which have recently occurred in Trafalgar-Square and of the danger to the peace of the Metropolis from meetings held there:-

And, with a view to prevent such disorderly proceedings and to preserve the public peace

I, CHARLES WARREN, the Commissioner of Police of the Metropolis, do hereby give Notice, with the sanction of the Secretary of State, and the concurrence of the Commissioners of Her Majesty's Works and Public Buildings, that until further intimation no Public Meetings will be allowed to assemble in Trafalgar-square, nor will speeches be allowed to be delivered therein: and all well-disposed persons are hereby cautioned and requested to abstain from joining or attending any such Meeting or Assemblage; and notice is further given that all necessary measures will be adopted to prevent any such Meeting or Assemblage, or the delivery of any speech, and effectually to preserve the Public peace and to suppress any attempt at the disturbance thereof.

This notice is not intended to interfere with the use by the public of Trafalgar-square for all ordinary purposes, or to affect the regulations issued by me with

respect to Lord Mayor's day.
CHARLES WARREN
The Commissioner of Police of the Metropolis.

As well as dutifully printing the warning poster *The Times* also reported on the chaos that had ensued the previous night. While the police were clearing the square they, and the London Samaritan Society, had handed out tickets for a night's lodging in the Casual Ward of the Endell Street Workhouse in Covent Garden.

But there had been insufficient room at the workhouse for the three hundred homeless who turned up and a riot had almost ensued. Now, the workhouse clerks were demanding more protection from the dreadfully overstretched police.

It seemed to Best that every solution tried threw up more problems. He blamed the Press for a lot of this. They encouraged the mob and the organisers by excitedly reporting their every move.

Indeed, for weeks now *The Times* had published a daily column entitled: *The Police and The Mob* (a title which Best felt betrayed a certain bias) which relayed in great detail all the previous day's activities in Trafalgar Square.

Sometimes this was of use to the police of course. For example, in today's issue, they described the clearing of the square and also the statements of the speaker, 'Comrade George' before he was removed from the speakers' platform. He, they declared, had 'the appearance of an Irishman and a red flag pinned to his breast'. He may have, but in fact Best knew he was an American citizen.

Comrade George's remarks had both amused Best and given him some pause. Instead of attacking the likes of Albert as one of Warren's Wolves he had complained about the 'enormous number of detectives being employed against them.'

At his lodging-house, Comrade George declared, about a hundred detectives had applied for beds. Best had smiled at this. Would that they had so many to spare!

'But the unemployed at the workhouse have kept watch,' the man said, 'to make sure that no bombs were left under their beds like the ones found in the Chicago cells.'

There were angry shouts at this. The finding of these in the cells of the condemned Haymarket bombers had, it was said, hardened the heart of the State Governor who might otherwise have commuted their sentences. Worse, their supporters were claiming that the police themselves had planted the bombs in the cells to ensure the men were hanged.

But Best frowned when he read Comrade George's final statement. It was a worrying one and was obviously meant to be.

"The unemployed, too, have their detectives,' he had announced with a grin, 'and they give us access to papers and information at Scotland Yard which tell us what the police are going to do.'

Was that true? Or merely mischief making?

Best sighed. One thing was certain. The anger and the resentments were building up and, he couldn't help feeling, something terrible was going to happen soon. Not, God help them, a bombing like Chicago. The Fenians had left their share of bombs around London but it was a long time since the loss of life had been anything near that of the Haymarket Riot.

24

Arthur Cooper sat outside his tent "chinning the cost" or, in plain English, cutting and whittling a stick to make a clothes peg.

Several other men were similarly employed as they sat on their caravan steps or in front of their tents. A number of children played in among the tents and caravans of the Wandsworth gypsy encampment but Best could see only one woman. Presumably the others were out selling the pegs, skewers and bunches of lavender, and telling fortunes.

Arthur Cooper struck Best as a ridiculously English sounding name for the dark-skinned Romany who glanced up when he stopped in front of him. He looked Best up and down slowly then said in a not unfriendly fashion, 'Jake Bosvil sent you.'

Best nodded.

'He told me you were looking for me and that you'd be by.'

Well that was a relief. In one sense. No need to explain himself or wheedle his way past all the gypsy suspicion of Gorgios never mind of policemen. On the other hand, if the man had anything to hide, he would be well prepared by now.

How astute of Jake to say that Best was looking for him. Made it appear that *he* had not named the man.

Cooper rose to his feet, brushed the wood chippings from his trousers, folded back the door covering and said, 'Come in,' extending his hand to guide Best into the oblong tent.

Best was surprised by the lack of antagonism and suspicion in the man's voice. Jake had done his job well.

Cooper, who was broadly made but a little less than middle height, had little problem entering the tent but Best had almost to bend double.

When his had eyes adjusted to the dim light he noticed that the tent contained little furniture, certainly no tables or chairs. Indeed, the only substantial object was a black, iron pot with perforations in its side, which was held off the ground by three legs: the fireplace. Alongside it was a bucket of the coke apparently not lately used the embers having died down.

Cooper led Best past the small piles of cooking pots and utensils which lined the tent's inner walls to a mattress, spread with a green coverlet, on the ground at the far end. He pointed to it, crossed his legs and squatted down all in one movement. Best struggled to execute a similar manoeuvre.

'Jake told me it's about Adeline,' he said when Best had sorted out his legs and got settled if not exactly comfortable.

Best nodded.

'I was sorry to hear her husband died. I wanted her and he won her but I was glad to see her happy.'

Somehow Best believed him. There was an air of simple goodness about the man and contentment with his lot.

As if to answer Best's unspoken question Cooper added, 'I was very taken with Adeline but I've found me a good wife and am happy now.'

'Then there was no bad feeling? When Myers got her?'

Cooper shook his head and smiled ruefully.

'She was a prize. But I think she would be needing a man more fired up than me. So, it was a blessing in the end, I suppose.'

Interesting.

'And this George Deighton. He wasn't fired up enough either?'

Cooper grimaced and shook his head. 'He was not the man for Adeline. Too crude. No brains.' He paused then said carefully. 'I don't know that much about him because he isn't a Romany.'

'Oh?,' said Best, 'He's a Choredo then? 'Or one of the Hindity-mengres?'

Cooper raised his eyebrows and gave Best a wry grin.

Helen had schooled Best on the identity of the travellers held in contempt by the Romanies who considered themselves the *real* gypsies. The Chorodies, she had explained, were regarded by them as a crude, squalid and dishonest people. English vagabonds, rogues and outcasts from way back they were originally of Saxon stock so tended to be fairer in appearance than the Romanies.

'That's when you can see their hair and faces for the grime. They're mostly tinkers and basket weavers although some "peel the stick" like the Romanies.'

The Hindity-mengre on the other hand were vagrant Irish, Helen explained. Many fewer in number than the Chorodies they were judged by the Romanies to be almost as repellent in their personal habits but regarded as having more native intelligence and cunning. Rather than whittle sticks to make skewers or weave baskets they spent their time making pots, pans and fake gold rings with which to deceive the gullible house-dwellers.

'Deighton is a Choredo, an English vagabond.'

'And he took her refusal badly?'

'So they say.'

'Especially because Myers was a Gorgio - a non gypsy?'

Cooper laughed out loud at that. 'Oh, no! The Chorodies don't *see* themselves as *gypsies*. They tell you, "We are not gypsy rubbish - nor Irish! *We are English!*"'

'I'm glad you told me that,' laughed Best. 'I've got to go to see him when he gets in to Latimer Road.'

'No need,' said Cooper. 'He's here.'

Best was puzzled. 'But Jake said he'd be going in there.'

Cooper shrugged. 'The Notting Dale site might be full. Or he could be having a feud with someone there.'

He jumped to his feet all in one movement as though propelled by elastic. 'If you're done with me, I'll show you where he is.'

Best unfolded himself more slowly, carefully straightening his knees and rubbing his legs to restore the feeling before turning to place a hand on the ground to push himself upright.

'My age is starting to show,' he apologised and grinned although it was not a cheerful thought.

'Nah,' said Cooper kindly. 'You're just not used to sitting like that.' He led the way to the tent flap.

'Over there.' He pointed over to the right where a group of ramshackle caravans huddled together against a wall. 'That lot are all Chorodies. Deighton's caravan is the one in the middle with the cracked chimney pot and broken steps. And there he is.'

A stocky, handsome, but exceedingly unkempt and filthy man with dark, curly black hair was emerging from the interior as they spoke. As he did so he turned his head and shouted coarsely to someone inside. Obviously not receiving the reply he wanted he slammed the door behind him causing the insubstantial vehicle to rock and lean even further to one side.

Still scowling, Deighton plonked himself down on the third step from the bottom, grabbed a nearby sack and took out a large knife. It was, Best noted, neither a garbling knife nor a kirpan.

He did not look up when Best approached although the detective was certain he was aware of his presence. He kept his head down and continued to rummage in the sack, extracting a hammer and various other tools.

'Mr Deighton?' enquired Best when it was obvious the man was not going to acknowledge him voluntarily.

Deighton's head came up sharply. 'Yes! Who wants him?'

Best began to explain who he was and his purpose even although Deighton had already ceased looking at him and rudely turned his head away. Suddenly, he made a disgusting hawking sound in his throat, filled his mouth and spat, only just missing Best's right foot.

At that moment, the caravan door opened and a dishevelled, grizzling, filthy little girl of about six years emerged. Her hair was black and curly like her father's but she was very pale apart from the red patches in the centre of her cheeks - as if she had been slapped.

She saw Best and began to run down the steps towards him, holding out her shivering, filthy hand.

The Detective Inspector stepped back in horror and before she could reach him turned and ran as if the devil were at his heels. No sign of stiffness now holding him back now. Nothing on earth could have stopped him.

25

Helen was startled to see her agitated husband dashing up their garden path at midday. She put down her paintbrush and went to greet him but he pushed past her muttering, 'I must bathe, I must bathe.'

She was even more startled by his reaction when Lucy, having heard his voice, appeared and began to run towards him.

'Stop her! Stop her!' he shouted. 'Don't let her near me. Take her away!'

When she had removed a tearful Lucy, Helen hurried back to demand, 'What on earth's going on!' although she had already half guessed.

'There was a little girl down at the encampment.'

Helen held up her hand to stop him.

'Joseph.'

He nodded miserably. The name brought back painful memories for them both. What happened to Joseph had caused Best to leave Helen and even when they were eventually reunited it was something they never discussed.

'She was shivering,' exclaimed a still agitated Best, 'her face was ashen but her cheeks were bright red!'

'Did she have a rash?'

He looked uncertain but said, 'I'm sure there was one around her neck.'

'With little points on it?'

He shook his head, then nodded. 'Yes. Yes. I'm sure.' Then sighed and admitted. 'I don't know. I don't know.' He hung his head. 'I just turned and ran.'

'That's understandable. Very understandable.'

She wanted to go over and comfort him but he backed away at her approach.

Best had taken over the care of Joseph when he and the young boy turned out to be among the very few survivors of the Princess Alice disaster. Joseph's parent had been among the hundreds drowned when the pleasure steamer sank after a collision in the Thames.

He had placed him into Helen's care when he was called away on a case.

She, thinking the bereaved child would benefit from the company of other little children, sent him to stay with her sister who had a large family. Her sister's children had played with him nicely and kept him company all right but had also passed scarlet fever on to him. He, being the weakest, had succumbed.

A distraught Best had blamed his death on Helen and it had taken another tragedy to reunite them.

Now they had their own child, his darling Lucy, Best became obsessed with protecting her from illness. He had nightmares sometimes about the number of evil diseases which seemed to be lying in wait for her: scarlet fever, diphtheria, typhoid, whooping cough, measles, smallpox. The list was endless. He was most afraid of being the one to bring them home to her.

'You won't just be leaving it at that?' Helen asked him carefully after he had bathed and sent his clothes to be disinfected. 'Another epidemic at a gypsy encampment would be disastrous.'

'I know. I know. 'I'll warn the medical authorities.'

'What about Deighton?'

'I don't *care* about my murder enquiry!'

She looked at him. 'You don't really mean that.'

He shrugged. 'All right. But I'm not going down there again.'

'You could. If they find it's clear of the disease.' She paused, then said gently. 'You know you would never forgive yourself ... '

'If there was another murder? I know, I know.' He shrugged. 'I think I was wasting my time with Deighton anyway. I could tell I wasn't going to get anything out of him without arresting him and I'd need some evidence against him to do that.'

The middle-aged man with the wild eyes, torn pea jacket and bandaged wrists, was trying to attract the attention of leading SDF member, John Burns, as he descended from his speakers' box at Hyde Park after making another fiery speech on behalf of the unemployed.

First the man spoke to Burns, then grabbed his arm but Burns shook him off and walked away through the cheering crowd, leaving him angry. He shouted after him, 'You've ruined me, you bastard. And you don't care! You've ruined me!'

He moved forward to give chase but Albert stepped in his path and grasped his upper arms so as not to injure his bandaged wrists further.

'And you're just as bad!' he spat at Albert. 'Helping them! Helping them make their speeches and rouse that stinking mob!'

He tried to pull away but Albert was too strong for him and tightened his grip. The man's head wove from side to side as he tracked Burns's progress through the congratulatory crowd. Albert waited until the SDF member was well out of sight before relaxing his grip.

How sad it was, thought Albert, that the ban on meetings in Trafalgar Square had not come sooner. If it had, then this poor man might not be off his head now.

It was right what they said. The Home Secretary had dragged his heels refusing to forbid the meetings but now that important bankers, businessmen, hoteliers and shopkeepers were pressing him to uphold the temporary ban he had assured them that it would stay.

He even announced that, strictly speaking, the square was not a public place. That, in fact, Trafalgar Square belonged to the Crown having originally been the site of the Royal Mews where Kings and Queens, from Henry the Fifth onwards, had stabled their horses. The public had been allowed to use it as a concession, he declared. A concession which could be withdrawn.

Fine time, thought Albert, to discover *that*. Too late for people like this poor fellow.

Albert's hopes that this revelation might bring an end to the mayhem which held the centre of London to ransom were suddenly dashed by the next speaker. To roars of approval he announced that a Monster Public Meeting would be held in Trafalgar square this very Sunday.

He urged all present to attend to defy the ban on meeting there, to protest the imprisonment of Irish M.P. Mr O'Brien, and to demonstrate the public's right to hold meetings whenever and wherever they liked.

In other words, Albert sighed, to defy police who would be obliged to try to stop them.

The man, who was still struggling to escape Albert's firm grip, was further agitated by this news and the delighted reaction of the crowd. To calm him down before finally releasing him and to defend himself against any accusation of officiousness Albert asked him for his name although he already knew it. He was Joseph Paxton.

He gave the name without demure but when it came to his address he began shouting again.

'I haven't got an address! I haven't got one! And it's all their fault!' He pointed angrily at the current speaker before dissolving into tears and pulling frantically at his bandages.

A burly man, wearing a red badge, turned around and yelled, 'If you don't you shut up I'll bloody well *make* you!'

'We want to listen to *him* – not you!' bellowed another.

A third man claimed, 'He's a police spy come to make trouble. That's what he is!'

At that, others began looking round angrily, muttering and raising their fists.

It's no good, Albert realised, I will have to take him into custody for his own protection and the safety of the public. He told Paxton what he was going to do but the man's attention was elsewhere.

With his free hand Albert began the usual procedure of patting his prisoner down to check whether he had anything on him with which he could injure himself or others. When his hand reached Joseph's right hand jacket pocket it stopped. He glanced over to a fellow constable and inclined his head towards his prisoner.

P C McCullough who, like so many Metropolitan Police officers was hardy Scot from the Highlands, instantly read Albert's unspoken request for assistance and came over. He held Joseph firmly while Albert extracted the suspect article from his prisoner's pocket. It was a short, squat-bladed dagger with a lethal point and an elaborately carved black handle and sheath with silver mounts etched with Celtic knots.

'That's a skean dhu,' muttered McCullough 'and a pretty ancient one at that.'

She was walking fast down Commercial Street. That pleased Stark because it meant she was not paying attention to people around or behind her. As long as she didn't change her usual route. That would throw his plain awry.

So far, there were no signs of her doing so. She passed the Ten Bell's Public House, crossed Fournier Street at a rush not even sparing her usual appreciative glance for the magnificent Christ Church designed by Nicholas Hawkesmoor for the Huguenot worshippers who had now mostly left the area.

The bitch did hesitate, however, by The Queen's Head on the next corner where she seemed to recognise one of the young prostitutes drunkenly emerging with a customer.

Don't be diverted into to trying to save the girl, he pleaded. She hesitated for a moment then nodded to the girl and gave the man a disapproving glance.

At Flower and Dean Street she turned left. He heaved a sigh of relief and even permitted himself a small smile. Everything was going to plan.

26

Best stared out of the window of the Inspectors' room at Scotland Yard wondering what he should do next. It stung him to recall the hoots of startled laughter which had followed his swift departure from the Wandsworth gypsy encampment.

Deighton would take that as a sign of weakness or even fear. His flight had certainly closed off that avenue of enquiry simply because he just could not bring himself to go back. Nothing would make him endanger the health of Lucy and Helen who were his life. A life which, after the death of his first wife from tuberculosis, and murder of his fiancé, had once not seemed worth living any more.

As for Deighton, he might appear antagonistic and intractable but, despite what he had told Helen, pressure could have been put upon him. If necessary he could have charged him with obstructing police in the execution of their duty. But contact with him would mean more risk of disease and in any case, if he did talk, he would doubtless lie.

He put the man out of his mind for the moment and decided to concentrate on the other possible suspects in the murder of a seemingly spotless member of the SDF and calling foreman at the London Dock.

Was that where the answer lay after all? Among the foreign ships, exotic cargoes and desperate casual labourers who might feel they had good reason to hate Myers because he had turned them down when they had begged for work?

Had one of them seen him in the square preaching fairness, equality and jobs for all and become incensed by his apparent hypocrisy?

Or was it the other way around? Had the Bessarabians failed to corrupt the man and killed him to keep his mouth shut and as a warning to others? The gang were certainly capable of that.

Armed with knives, guns and broken bottles, they not only terrorised the mainly Russian Jewish shopkeepers and small workshop owners with demands for protection money but went in for blackmail drawing up lists of potential victims. These, oddly, even included the families of prospective brides whom they approached threatening to expose the girl's supposed sexual indiscretions.

Their victims, having an in-built fear of police and gang retribution, rarely reported them. Matters had been made worse by a vigilante group formed to resist them, the Odessians, who had now gone into the protection business themselves.

Had Myers been on the Bessarabians blackmail list – or even that of the Odessians - and refused to pay up or allow them access into the promisingly lucrative London Dock?

But, if one of these gangs *had* killed Myers, why had they not advertised the fact to take advantage of the fear engendered? Perhaps they had - at the docks - or why would their name have surfaced there? He sighed and thought I better go down there again.

Then there was the question of whether the influence of share-owning Mrs Myers had got her husband the job – which in turn might have made ferocious enemies among his colleagues? Killing him might be an extreme reaction but in places where violence was commonplace it began to seem less heinous; a more legitimate way to settle a resentment.

Or, then again, ludicrous as it may seem, had the in-fighting among the SDF and the other socialist organisations suddenly been raised to murderous levels?

He frowned. The motives all seemed somehow unconvincing to him even given that motives for murder were often trivial to the outsider's eye. Usually, one lead would have jumped out at him as the most likely. But none had.

Who knows, he prodded himself, something quite unexpected might turn up any minute and change everything?

If only he had John George Smith to talk things over with. Albert was keen but inexperienced and not good at making up his mind. But Sergeant Smith, with whom he had thrashed out many a tricky case, was otherwise engaged as, it seemed, was everyone else at the moment.

Well, I must do *something* he decided and stood up resolutely though still undecided. He smiled to himself thinking, I've been infected with Albert's disease.

That was unfair. Albert *had* done something on his own initiative and cleared up an important problem. He had rushed up to Best as he passed through the square grinning and exclaiming, 'The bangle. I've found out about the bangle!'

Best had patted the air in a calming motion and got him to begin at the beginning, but soon regretted doing so.

'I got to thinking about it when I was standing here,' Albert said breathlessly, 'it was partly the broken safety chain and partly because he didn't seem to be the sort of bloke to have another woman him being so busy and having such a nice wife, you said.'

'And . . .?' encouraged Best.

'Well, I thought maybe it was just something simple. Nothing dodgy about him having that bangle after all. You told me to look at the obvious things first, so I did. Then it came to me. What if he had just found it in the street? Put it in his pocket to give to a policeman or take it to the station?'

Best looked at him dazedly then smacked his own forehead. 'You looked in the Property Lost Book.'

Albert nodded eagerly. 'And there it was. Lost in the square by a young woman from Plaistow on the same night as Myers was murdered.'

'You put me to shame,' said Best, patting him on the arm. '*I* should have thought of that.'

'Oh, no,' said Albert. 'You can't think of *everything*. You're very busy and I got nothing to do except stand here and think.'

The idea of Albert now comforting him amused Best.

'Right,' he said, 'I want you to just stand there and think about the diary entry: what was the man thinking of leaving? Then, think about who committed the murder? And the case will be solved.' He smiled the dazzling smile that Albert had not seen for quite a while, patted his arm and exclaimed, 'Good work!'

Albert couldn't stop grinning. His goal seemed so much nearer.

Best's train of thought was disturbed by a sharp a knock on the office door. A telegraph clerk opened it and put his head around announcing with unnecessary brusqueness, 'Urgent message for you, sir,' and thrust the form at him. He knew they were very busy now but did they have to sound so peremptory?

The message, from Albert at Hyde Park Police Station, was a masterpiece of brevity and mystery and quite uncharacteristic of the young constable. It read simply: 'Come quickly. Important.'

Briskness was in the air it seemed. But, he shrugged. Why not do as Albert demanded? Encourage this new decisiveness. The alternatives were so unpromising.

Stark wasn't the only one reliving that night. It was often on Florence's mind but especially so now. One of the young girls soliciting outside the Cambridge Theatre had put her in mind of Jenny. Jolly Jenny. It was the way the girl had thrown back her head and laughed raucously at something a man had said. She recalled again Jenny seizing her Army bonnet, clamping it to her head and marching up and down alternately banging an imaginary drum and shaking a pretend tambourine, the way the *Hallelujah Sisters*: *Happy Eliza* and *Converted Jane* did at the music hall.

It had been fun, she now saw, being with someone so alive and carefree. Or, at least, apparently carefree.

Only when Jenny had fallen sick and Florence nursed her had she discovered that the cheeky grin masked a bruised soul. And that had set Florence off on a mission to mend it. To save the girl for Jesus – and herself.

The night she had gone to start her on the path to giving herself to the Lord had been a similar one to this. Bleak, a faint chill in the air and the moon hiding behind heavy clouds most of the time.

Despite this, Florence had been alive with hope and expectation when she ascended the tenement stairs on her way to collect Jenny. She tried to block out of her mind the scene which had greeted her when she reached Jenny's bleak and bare room. But it kept resurfacing: Jenny spread out obscenely on her bed, her throat cut and blood seeping from the stab wounds to her still warm body. And beside her – she could not bear to remember what had lain beside her - nor face again that this might be all her fault.

She was walking fast again, looking neither to left nor right, but then she always did when she was in this area. He knew bad memories reached out to her there. Serves her right, the interfering bitch trying to take away his livelihood like that.

His life had never been the same since either. On the run. Always looking over his shoulder. But that would end soon. Very soon. Only this bonneted bible pounder stood in the way of his getting his life back to the way it had been before that night.

It had been from Jenny's friend, Mabel, that they had learned about Stark, a man who had once been her pimp. A man who had raped her as a child and kept a hold on her afterwards. Eventually, she had managed to escape and set up on her own.

But he found her and kept trying to reinstate himself as her 'protector' but, said Mabel, Jenny had resisted. Fought him off with a fury.

'She was stronger after you began helping her.'

Florence's sadness was compounded by the knowledge that Jenny had never even hinted about her difficulties with this man and she thought, I didn't help her much, did I, if she couldn't tell me that?

'She never told no-one but me,' Mabel had explained trying to reassure Florence. But it didn't. 'She thought he might start going for you,' she explained. 'She was protecting you.'

That made Florence feel even worse and set her to wondering whether she was really fit for this kind of work. Wasn't *she* supposed to be the one doing the protecting?

Neither Best, who had seen the man fleetingly in a poor light, nor the local police, who had never heard of him, had been able to trace Stark. Florence was the only person who had seen him at close quarters. She refused to desert her other two women she visited in Rye Court but was now about to enter the alleyway in some trepidation and always put it off until the end of her rounds.

27

Albert was sitting on a bench in Hyde Park Police Station charge room looking very pleased with himself.

'Well, what have you got that's so important?' asked Best as he sat down beside him.

Albert could scarcely conceal his glee.

'The murderer.'

'Oh, Yes?' said Best raising his eyebrows questioningly.

If only he was right! What a relief that would be. But the lad was inexperienced and his enthusiasm could easily carry him away. Then again, Albert was not one to reach such a stunning conclusion without entering into prolonged discussions on the subject with his colleagues. Maybe he *had* found the murderer, Best thought hopefully, but prepared himself for disappointment.

'Come on then, tell me about it,' he said. 'From the beginning.'

Albert told him about Joseph Paxton's attempts to reach the speakers, his fury at them, and the finding of the knife.

'But,' said Best, 'that was in Hyde Park and the murder took place in Trafalgar Square.'

Albert nodded excitedly. 'Yes, but Paxton had been doing the same things down there. Causing a commotion and getting angry because his business was ruined. You see he had owned *Paxton's Curiosities*, an antique shop almost overlooking the square. At least he had until his clients were frightened away by the mob. He became destitute, homeless and obsessed by letting these agitators know what they had done to him.'

Best put up his right hand to stop the flow.

'Why,' he said stiffly, 'have I not heard about this man before?'

Albert's grin began to fade and was replaced by a puzzled frown. Then, when the portent of the question dawned on him, a look of abject apology.

'Yes, well . .' he stumbled, 'Well, you know how it is, we get lots of people like him – nutters - wandering about the ground and turning up at the station. We scarcely notice them and . . .'

'*People like him?*' exclaimed Best cuttingly. 'Whose businesses have been ruined by the mob and want revenge on the speakers?'

Albert hesitated then said, 'Well, maybe not *exactly* like him.'

'People who would have access to curios and antique knives?'

'Well, no, perhaps. I don't know,' he finished lamely, his head down.

Best gazed at him in silence for a moment then took a deep breath. 'Look, I'm pleased with what you've done and I'll be absolutely delighted if he *is* the murderer but if you want to be a detective you've got to remember to think beyond what's in front of you. Use this.' He tapped Albert on the forehead.

Albert nodded forlornly.

'You should have told me about Joseph Paxton, shouldn't you?'

Albert shrank lower in his seat and nodded.

'Why?'

'Because he has a motive?'

'Yes.'

'What else?'

'The means.'

'Yes.'

'You should have told me about him.'

'I know,' whispered Albert seeing his dreams of Yard glory disappearing.

Best patted Albert's hand. 'But, of course, a motive and means are not enough. You need proof. So tell me, what proof makes you so sure that he stabbed Mr Myers to death?'

Albert sat forward, clasping his hands together and looking Best in the eye. 'He confessed.'

Best raised his eyebrows again and laughed. 'Well, I have to admit that's a promising sign. But as you know a great many people confess even to things they have not done and you *did* say he was not right in the head.' He paused. 'Anything else?'

Albert nodded vigorously and this time couldn't keep the grin from spreading all over his face. 'He knew the weapon was a kirpan.'

At this, Best closed his eyes for a moment. They had not revealed this fact to anyone. When he opened his eyes his face was also lit up with a grin. He slapped Albert on the back.

'Good man!' he exclaimed. 'Good man!'

They grinned at each other, triumphantly.

As usual, the darkness was almost total or would have been if it had not been whitened by the thickening fog. She could only sense the tall buildings looming sinisterly on either side of her turning Rye Court into a blind-ended tunnel.

As usual, she moved carefully, aware of the rocky paving stones and ragged holes which could cause her to fall any moment. Tonight she listened particularly hard for sounds nearby but could hear only her own hollow footsteps. She comforted herself that perhaps if *she* couldn't see anyone wishing her ill then *they* would not be able to see her either.

As her eyes became a little adjusted to the dark and the fog, she caught the tiniest glimpse of light from a hovel to her left. That meant that number seventeen Rye Court was just ahead. Despite the fact that, with the nights getting colder, she was now obliged to wear her cape she found herself shivering and was relieved to see the house she was seeking.

Once again, she climbed the cold, bleak stone stairs to the first floor taking care not to grip the shaky handrail too firmly. On the landing, she knocked gently on the second door to the left and entered.

Inside was much as it always was. Lizzie Carter, wrapped in a shawl to keep out the cold, sitting at the table surrounded by boxes, stamens, wire and artificial flower petals their vivid colours almost mocking the woman's pallid face and the dire surroundings.

As always, Lizzie's fingers did not stop moving as she raised her head to greet Florence but, Florence was delighted to see, there was no sign of new bruises and there was even a ghost of a smile on the woman's face. Now, *that* was unusual. Had her scheme worked? Earned Lizzie a respite?

On her last visit Florence had had a word with Boris, Lizzie's husband, voicing her concerns about the woman. Had Lizzie been getting into fights with other women, she had asked him? Was that what was causing all these bruises? If so, had they better tell the police? She had taken care not to give the slightest hint that Lizzie had told her how she acquired her injuries, and indeed, she hadn't.

He had claimed to be as perplexed as she so Florence had asked his help in keeping an eye on his wife and given him two shillings to buy her a tonic. She knew full well where the money would go and it made them short on their own housekeeping not to mention being against the rules. But, if the hope of further donations gave Lizzie a respite, it was worth it. Just to see that glimmer of a smile and a glimpse of the woman she once was.

Sometimes, Florence hoped, if the men realised that the results of their brutality towards their wives was at least being noticed, they might feel a little shame. At least enough to make them keep their fists to themselves for a short while.

Florence and Lizzie sat for a while making flowers together while she told Lizzie of the goings on in that outside world: of the Jubilee celebrations, the Queen's presents, marches, meetings and speeches. She even managed to make her laugh once about the silliness of men.

Big Joe Benbow was a man who would not harm a single hair on the head of his beloved wife Elsa. He watched her constantly but out of love and concern not anger or jealousy. What concerned this man with shoulders and neck made massive by gruelling hard work at the docks – when he could get it – was the delicate health of the fair and childlike Elsa and that of their twin sons.

Up until now the chances of him getting regular work had been minimal. They had reached desperation point. Were fighting off that final defeat; the workhouse which meant separation and despair. But here there *had* been a change. A considerable change.

A proper fire crackled in the grate, two oil lamps lit up the meagre room rather than the usual guttering candle stumps and, as Florence arrived, they were about to enjoy a proper meal of beef and vegetables. Florence, their guardian angel, was urged to sit down and share in their good fortune.

Had Joe turned to crime, Florence worried? She could hardly blame him if he had. He grinned at her when she made a tentative enquiry about their new circumstances – the first time she had ever seen him smile.

'What it is,' he said, 'is that Bert Hardy – he's one of the new calling foremen at the London Docks since Mr Myers died - he was finding things a bit hard to sort out. Keeping a grip on it an all. So,' he said triumphantly 'so they took me on as his assistant.'

'How wonderful!'

'Aye', Joe paused then said with an understandable note of pride, 'They said they wanted someone what was trustworthy, experienced, a good worker and able to stand up to the hard men.' He grinned again. 'Course I already knew Bert, we'd worked together a while back, over at the Surrey Docks.'

To please them Florence ate a little of beef and vegetables and revelled in their obvious relief and delight at being able to give something back and not having to go out begging or selling what was left of their pots and pans and clothes to be able to feed their young lads. Misery was Florence's usual daily diet so she was overwhelmed with delight at seeing such evident happiness.

However one thought kept nagging. Would it last? What would happen when Bert Hardy had learned the ropes? But she couldn't ask that. Let them enjoy their happy moment.

Joe read her mind. 'They've promised that when old Bert is sorted out and they don't need me no more to help him I'll get taken on as one of the permanent men.'

Elsa gazed at him proudly, pulling her new pink and black shawl around her shoulders even though the room was warm enough for once.

'You must take some of this with you,' muttered Joe pointing to the joint. He had never ceased being grateful at how Florence's small contributions had kept them from starving and her attention had kept Elsa from total despair. 'Help out some of your other people.'

Elsa, new colour in her cheeks and hope in her eyes, nodded vigorously. Florence accepted gratefully. She had called on an old couple earlier and been mortified that she could only offer them a small cheese sandwich between them. It was all she had had left and they had pretended it was more than enough because old people didn't need so much food.

Before she left Joe sliced off a large chunk of the juicy meat, wrapped it carefully in a clean cloth, handed it to her and offered to escort her to the end of the court. She was tempted to accept. She felt unusually nervous tonight but could not bring herself to break up their celebratory meal just because she was having a silly fit of nerves.

Hadn't she been here dozens of times since that terrible night? Nothing had happened then. So why should it now? She was missing Albert and was miserable without him. That was it.

After she said her goodbyes and begun descending the murky stone stairs she heard raised voices from the floor above: a man and woman having a row. The man's voice was thunderous and threatening. The woman's a blend of fear and end-of-her-tether anger. Florence wished they would be quiet so she could listen for other sounds: creaking and rustling and heavy breathing that might warn her of an impending attack.

How silly she was being. Attack by whom? That business with Jenny might have happened nearby but that had been many months ago. The man had fled never to be seen again. Well, not as far as she knew. No-one around here had admitted to even knowing him.

Apart from Jenny's friend, Mabel, and she had never actually seen the man. Had no idea what he looked like, where he lived or whether Stark was his real name.

'Before it happened I sometimes wondered whether he was real,' Mabel had confided. 'Cos Jenny could be a bit of a romancer you know. But,' she had added tearfully, 'that was nothing to romance about, was it? That man terrorising her?'

She did know that Jenny had once discovered Stark 'trying it on' with little Annie Jessop from the rooms below. 'He'd broken into Jenny's room and been there when little Annie came up to see her. She told him if she caught him at it again she'd go to the police.'

Apparently, she *had* caught him at it again and that, it seemed, was why both of them, Jenny and Annie, had been found laying side by side, battered, bloodied and dead, on Jenny's bed that night.

The only person who had actually seen Stark, or a man running from the scene, if that was who it was, and only fleetingly, was Inspector Best. And, of course, she herself. It was she who had got the closest view.

She gripped the stair rail tightly, leaning heavily on it as if to reassure herself. Suddenly it moved under her grip and came away from the wall. She toppled forward, grabbing wildly for support, her satchel falling from her shoulders and pulling her downward several steps. Then the bag stopped falling and its bulky pad halted her fall.

She was spread-eagled, head down, legs up, skirt around her waist in a most inelegant fashion. If the General could see her now he wouldn't be so sure about her suitability for higher things! She almost giggled at the thought. But she was very shaken and as the initial shock subsided she began to hurt in several places. She took a moment to get her breath back, turn herself around, pull her skirt down and, pushing against the wall, regain her feet. She brushed herself down with her hands then checked for damage. Her palms were stinging and were filthy and grazed and she had banged her right knee. But it was her left ankle that really hurt. Oh, dear.

Thank you God for saving me, she thought, although you might have saved my ankle as well. Should she go back up and get help? No, she thought, I must get out of here – it's only a sprain. She began hobbling down the ill-lit stairs very slowly tentatively placing her right foot on each step and following it slowly and carefully with the left.

She was on the last landing. Only one more flight of stairs but as she reached them the wall light went out leaving blackness, complete blackness, the only sound her own breathing. Oh, God what should I do now, she thought. Try to get back upstairs to safety?

No, she was just being silly. It was nothing sinister. The oil must have run out of the lamp. Someone had forgotten to fill it. That was all. Spent the money on drink instead. It happened sometimes. She must get out, get back to the main streets where there was more light and people. She felt her way down the last flight, wincing all the way as her ankle began to throb.

Suddenly there were no more steps. She was there – the ground floor. She felt about with her right foot. No, no more steps. She had reached the ground floor. She sighed with relief.

Now all she had to do was turn right. The front door was dead ahead, she remembered that.

It was as she turned and stepped forward that she heard a swishing movement behind her and heavy breathing – and smelled that smell. Then a rough hand came around her mouth and another snaked around her body, crushing the breath out of her.

He had come to get her as she had always known he would.

28

It was the most awesome sight Albert had ever seen. He thought he had already experienced Trafalgar Square in every possible condition: rowdy with the mob; strewn with the sleeping bodies of the homeless in the dead of night and covered with litter after their departure. Then, during the last few days at least, blessedly peaceful, clean, free of tumult and peopled only by those out to see the sights and enjoy themselves.

But this was a startlingly new aspect: the surface of the square blanketed edge-to-edge with navy blue. He had never seen so many policemen together in one place. The mid-morning sun glinted off countless silver tunic buttons, helmet badges and stirrups. There must be over a thousand men here?

Officers were ranged two deep around three of the squares sides and four deep on the open south side, which had no stone balustrade to aid its defence. Squads of a hundred each blocked the steps down into the square at the northern corners, three hundred more police were drawn up alongside Nelson's column and another solid body stood at the South East corner. There were also a hundred mounted policemen in between the fountains.

Despite the vast numbers there was an eerie calm. All seemed aware that they were part of something momentous. That, after this, nothing would be the same. They were battle ready. Expectant. A little nervous.

Many were also very tired. The excess overtime during the lead up to this day had made their lives seem long on penance for sins they hadn't committed. Some could scarcely keep their eyes open having come straight from night duty or risen well before dawn and travelled miles from outer divisions to get here. The uncertainty about just when the square would be invaded did not help them stay alert.

A specified time for the forbidden Monster Meeting had been stated on the posters: 2.30pm. The speakers, chairmen and the resolutions to be adopted had also been duly tabled. But the timing of the marches, approaching now from every direction, had been deliberately kept secret. As had the numbers involved.

The posters had urged:

ATTEND IN TENS OF THOUSANDS!
PRESERVE YOUR DEARLY BOUGHT LIBERTIES!

Judging by the news coming in, tens of thousands were doing just that, and Trafalgar Square with more entry points than a bathroom sponge could not have been a harder place to defend. There were one or two routes in at every corner.

Already, Albert could hear the yells and the banging of drums coming from the north-west corner, where a march from the West was trying to break through, and the South East corner by The Strand, where East Enders led by John Burns were spearheading their invasion.

He knew about, but as yet could not yet see or hear the most dreaded of the columns, the one from the southeast. This had set out from Woolwich and headed along the south bank of the Thames picking up supporters in Plumstead, Deptford, Greenwich, Rotherhithe, Bermondsey, Southwark and Lambeth, and was now said to be ten thousand strong.

The march from Clerkenwell Green, full of fiery souls led by Annie Besant and William Morris, had also yet to appear. That one was expected to try to breech police defences from the North East corner by St Martin's Church.

The atmosphere throbbed with suspense as police and the watching crowd waited to see what would happen when all the thousands heading towards this point met police head on.

The feverishly expectant watching crowd grew larger by the minute and police had been instructed to keep them moving. Not a good idea, Albert thought. Those pushed back became angry, particularly when pushed back by the mounted police whose huge horses terrified them.

Adding to the sense of barely controlled chaos, omnibuses were driving round and round the square to give their passengers a good view of this exciting sight at sixpence a time. One or two of the marchers who had managed to break through and jump on board were haranguing police from the upper decks about their rights to free speech.

Another log had been thrown on the smouldering fire by the news from Chicago that four of the Haymarket accused had finally been hanged. A fifth had committed suicide by placing a fulminating cap – a detonator - in his mouth. This act was treated with great suspicion by many of his supporters. No-one, no matter how desperate, they believed, would commit suicide in such a fearful manner.

Even some of the watching crowds were angry about the executions or what the socialists were calling 'judicial murder'.

It's nothing to do with us, thought Albert, but it would be used by our enemies who say that all police are brutal. Warren's Wolves again.

There *were* other views. Some pointed out with admiration how much more sternly such matters were dealt with across the Atlantic.

Whatever we do, it's wrong, thought Albert before he went back to wondering they might get something to eat and drink.

At 1pm four squadrons of Life Guards rode down The Mall and turned into Horse Guards Parade where they settled and waited. In St George's Barracks conveniently situated just behind the National Gallery, four hundred Grenadier Guards, foot soldiers, also waited.

Their presence might be reassuring in one sense but Albert still could not see how so vulnerable a site could be defended without dreadful bloodshed. Pray God no-one would resort bombs in desperation as they had in Chicago's Haymarket.

There is no doubt we are a colourful sight, Best thought, as he marched along the south bank of the Thames behind a brass band, banners and a flurry of waving flags.

The socialists and anarchists were wearing red ribbons and armbands while the Irish National League sported gold and green caps, sashes and rosettes.

Best had realised that he also better show some sign of political allegiance even though he felt he had already gone beyond the call of duty by looking so dirty and unkempt. He had settled for a narrow red riband across his threadbare grey jacket. Wrinkled and dirty black fustian trousers, down-at-heel boots with a hole in the right toe and a grimy flat cap completed his ensemble.

When little Lucy had seen him before he left home that morning she had screamed with fright and hidden behind her mother's skirt. But Helen had scarcely been able to keep the smile from her lips at the sight of her usually immaculate husband.

He had taken care to infiltrate himself near the head of the march so that he could keep the leaders well in view, particularly those riding in the brakes up front. Surprises and diversionary tactics were expected in the battle to breach the square and it was these leaders who would orchestrate them.

Those who had joined the march early were tiring now. When the bands paused between rousing marches, they rallied themselves by singing their favourite songs; *Starving for Old England* and the *Marseillaise*. Their voices rose with particular fervour when they came to the final words, **Liberty or Death!**

The sight of her usually immaculate husband might have amused Helen when he left home in his threadbare suit, worn-down boots and grimy, flat cap, but she had also been afraid.

She had read about the determination of the socialists, radicals and anarchists to beat the police at all costs. To reassert their freedom to meet and march wherever and whenever they liked. She was sympathetic to their cause but also worried. Very worried.

Best was going right among them, in disguise, even pretending to be one of them. That was a very risky thing to do. What if someone recognised him? What if they turned on him in their rage and killed him. It had happened before.

She had not felt such fear since that terrible night when she had discovered that he had been on board the Princess Alice when it was rammed by a Tyne collier. Reports were coming through of hundreds drowned and she had not known whether he was among them. It made her tearful even now to recall catching sight of him standing there, in that terrible hall full of bodies waiting to be identified, with little Joseph clinging to his leg.

His clothing then, provided by a kindly gentleman's outfitter to replace his own filthy and sodden ones, had been similarly cheap and ill-fitting.

She tried to distract herself by working; laying down the initial outline of her picture of Lucy which she was painting for Earnest as a birthday surprise. But she was unable to concentrate.

She was gripping her paintbrush too hard. Her strokes were jerky. Lucy, sensing her mother's distraction, squirmed about on her chair and kept trying to climb down. Helen sighed and was scraping the paint off once again when she heard raised voices in the street outside and looked out.

Four dishevelled men, one bleeding from a wound on his head, were talking and gesticulating wildly to a group of open-mouthed passers-by who were hanging on to their every word.

Helen dashed out, not bothering to remove her smock, to join the listeners.

'It's murder there! It's war!' the injured man was saying. 'But we will beat the bastards. Even if we have to kill every one of them! We'll get through'

29

The sides of the square were now dense with spectators awaiting the big showdown. They lined the pavements and jostled each other for a better position on the steps of St Martins Church. The windows of Morley's Hotel and The Grand Hotel opposite the South East corner were packed with guests and staff vying for the best view.

Even more thunderous shouts and rallying cries could now be heard from the Strand corner but marchers were still being kept out of the square. The fighting in Waterloo Place by those trying to break through into Pall Mall and thus gain an entry into the north west corner had become even fiercer and a diversionary column was attempting to infiltrate from the adjacent Haymarket.

To the relief of Albert and his kind the chances of a major attack at the North East corner had been averted, the Clerkenwell Green march had, they were told, been cut off and dispersed as it approached down St Martin's Lane.

The Commissioner was still directing operations in the square and sending round his senior officers to pass on instructions to the men.

'The mobs are breaking up and trying to infiltrate in smaller numbers!' shouted Chief Constable Howard, as he drew near to where Albert stood cold, hungry and needing a pee. 'Be alert! Keep your eyes open!'

But it was not just smaller numbers. Ominous bulges kept appearing in their ranks down by the Strand. The police line swayed back and forward like an undulating snake as they repulsed sections of the mob who then tried to break through further along.

Suddenly there was a dramatic surge at one particular point. They were breaking through! Albert was among those who rushed forward to buttress the line. So were members of the mounted branch.

This frightened the angry crowd who began hooting, stoning them, throwing sticks, and trying to pull the riders from their mounts. They even struck out at the horses.

The noise was deafening, the air full of fury and hatred, the confusion awful. A rider-less police horse bucked and turned in confusion, a dismounted officer hung on to the reins of another horse. Albert helped him back onto his mount then turned to find himself face to face with the howling mob and it shocked him. They shoved one group back but the pressure building up from behind them was becoming irresistible.

With another determined push an unlikely couple broke through: the pugnacious working class SDF leader, John Burns, and the tall and picturesque Cunningham Graham, wealthy son of a Scottish laird and Member of Parliament. Another top-hat socialist.

Albert was not the only one who immediately recognised the pair. He soon lost sight of them as they were ambushed by his colleagues.

When they emerged from the melee they were being held firmly, the M.P. was bleeding from the head and, Albert was shocked to see some officers striking at them while they were being frogmarched into custody. Venting *their* fury, getting their own back, he supposed, for the continuous taunting, baiting and insults rained on them during the long, weary hours of duty that the actions of these men had brought about. For the blistered feet, soaking uniforms, hunger and utter exhaustion.

A violent shove rocked the distracted Albert and as he turned to repulse the new invaders he felt a stunningly painful blow to his face.

Through dazed eyes he saw a large fist being withdrawn. When he was able to focus again, his nose and cheeks were throbbing, he glanced round to find who had struck him but saw only the howling, cursing, mob. His nose felt wet. He put up his hand and it came away bloody.

What's this, thought Best as they approached Waterloo Bridge? We're slowing down. Almost coming to a halt. He glanced up to the front of the column. Oh damn. Bloody damn! The brake carrying the leaders had gone!

He stepped out of the line onto the pavement, pushed through the roadside crowd and jumped on a low wall. Over the heads of the crowd he caught sight of the brake galloping ahead. He pushed people aside and began to run, trying to keep the horse and cart in sight. But it was no good. They were going too quickly and the crowd was in his way. He watched them disappearing and cursed.

There had to be *some* way. He looked around for a horse and cart to commandeer. Just then an empty hansom cab emerged from a side-street and turned left, obviously trying to get ahead of the march. Best shouted to the cabbie, shot up his hand and ran towards it brandishing his warrant card. He jumped on board ignoring oaths from the surly driver. Fortunately, the man's fear of displeasing the police, who could block his licence, overcame any loyalty he might have to the marchers.

By now the brake had got well ahead. Despite the hansom's infinitely sleeker and lighter body and burden it was going to be difficult to catch up but Best kept shouting up to the driver urging him on until they caught sight of the brake and closed the distance between them.

The brake dashed onwards, pausing neither for Waterloo nor Westminster Bridges. Where were they going? What were they up to?

At last, as it approached Lambeth Bridge, it began to slow down.

'Slow down! Slow down!' Best shouted.

If they pulled up suddenly behind their quarry they would attract attention. 'Make your bloody mind up,' yelled the cabbie but obeyed.

The brake turned onto Lambeth Bridge and began to cross but came to an abrupt halt at the centre where a knot of similarly-garbed men had gathered.

The leaders of the Thameside march jumped from their cart and walked over to a tall man wearing a red and green top hat. There was much shaking of hands and slapping of backs then a hurried consultation began.

As they talked their lieutenants glanced around them suspiciously, on the alert for 'police spies'.

Best leaned back into what scant shadow the hansom cab afforded and kept talking to the cabbie, warning him of dire consequences should he reveal the identity of his passenger and ordering him to listen and reply as if he was receiving instructions regarding their route and possibly disputing the fare.

As the two groups of men conspired they gestured towards the south bank and ahead of them towards the Houses of Parliament. Pocket watches were consulted. Heads were shaken, then nodded. More gesturing.

While Best champed at the bit with frustration his attention was drawn to movement and noise from the far end of the bridge. He saw the north bank of the Thames black with people and bright with flags and banners: the South West London march!

Instantly, he realised what was happening. Knew what their plans were. The thought horrified him.

Hands were being shaken, farewells taken, the parties began to disperse and return to their respective columns.

Best urged the agitated cab driver forward to the north bank instructing him to cut across in front of the waiting South West London column, turn right and head for Parliament Square.

The man gazed unhappily at the waiting march.

'It's all right. You can do it!' shouted Best. 'They won't move off straight away!'

Objective achieved he kept up the pressure offering money now as well as threats.

'Come on! Come on!' he yelled. 'You'll get a big reward!'

When the sweating horse slowed at the police cordon Best leaped out and began to run, whipping off his grimy cap with one hand, pulling out his warrant card with the other, holding it aloft and waving it. He pushed through the police cordon and headed towards the mounted figure at the centre of the crossroads between Parliament Street and Bridge Street.

Shouts rang out as he ran.

'Hey! What the hell d'you think you're you doing!'

'Stop him! Stop him!'

Two constables darted forward ready to bring Best down. At that moment, Superintendent Dunlop saw what was happening, recognised Best, shouted 'Leave him!' and beckoned him forward.

'The two marches, they're timing it to arrive together!' Best panted. He pointed forward across the bridge and right from the way he had come.

'And there are *thousands* of them!'

Albert was only too pleased to be ordered to form up and quick march south towards Parliament Square. Anything was better than this standing around while thousands of spectators gathered eagerly waiting to you get bloodied.

One thing that Warren was keen on was them learning to march properly. They managed a particularly rapid quick march south from the square, skirted the statue of little Charles I on his big horse and, followed the path of the fated monarch's gaze, passing boarded-up banks and public houses.

'Move it! Move it!' yelled Inspector Barrett, a plump man who seemed to be having difficulty in keeping up himself.

As they sped along to their left was the alleyway leading into the Metropolitan Police Headquarters in Great Scotland Yard and Whitehall Place. To their right, the handsome, gated Palladium building of the Horse Guards. At that moment out rode two squadrons of Life Guards, a magnificent sight in their scarlet tunics, burnished breast plates and glowing helmets. Evidently the crowds agreed given the cheers which greeted the troupe as they approached Trafalgar Square.

'Come on! Come on! Pick 'em up there!' yelled Barrett, breathlessly urging them on past the elegant Banqueting House where King Charles I was beheaded.

By the time they reached Parliament Square they were breathless and perspiring heavily. In the shadow of Big Ben and rank upon rank of policemen were lined up, some facing westwards but most looking south towards Westminster Bridge.

'Blimey, what do they need *us* for?' puffed Eddie Clark, the overweight PC to Albert's left. 'There's hundreds of them here already!'

'Halt! Left, turn!' yelled Barrett, 'Stand easy!'

Albert relaxed and reached inside his tunic for his handkerchief to wipe his forehead and mop up the persistent trickle from his bloody nose. His hand froze midway.

'Oh, my gawd!' Clark exclaimed when he saw what was heading towards them.

The mob had broken through the blockade on the south side of the river and were now edge to edge crossing Westminster Bridge and approaching fast. With the sun behind them, flags and banners pointing forward; sticks, iron bars and lead piping shaken threateningly and wagons overflowing with angry, gesticulating figures they were an awesome sight.

Worst of all was the noise.

Like an invading hoard of Huns bent on terrifying their foes into submission they rent the air with their hoots and boos and yells, the insistent beat of their drums, and the relentless tread of thousands of pairs of boots.

'Victory or Death!' rang in the air.

'Draw your truncheons!' yelled Inspector Barrett.

'Oh, bloody hell,' whispered Albert.

30

The lone figure of Superintendent Dunlop was an impressive but slightly ludicrous figure as he rode out to meet the oncoming march, his right hand held up as though stopping vehicles at a busy crossroads rather than attempting to halt a defiant mob in sight of the very seat of government.

'Stop!' he shouted. 'In the name of the law!'

The mob ignored him - not even breaking step.

'Halt!' he yelled again. On they came.

Superintendent Dunlop, a veteran of many meetings and marches here on his division, had once declared that it would take a sterner heart than this to prevent poor, houseless creatures sleeping on the streets after wandering all day without food.

The deafening noise Albert heard from the front of him was now echoed on his right. Glancing over, his sweating hand tightening on his truncheon, he saw the advance guard of the South West London march bearing banners of the Lambeth Progressive and West Sussex Socialist Clubs. They, it seemed, did not intend to be halted either.

'Oh, my God,' he whispered.

Superintendent Dunlop made another futile attempt to stop the first march but when they were almost upon him and missiles began to rain down he admitted defeat. No sense in becoming another martyr.

News had already come through that an Inspector who had tried to halt an offshoot of the Strand crowd had been knocked unconscious with an iron bar.

Dunlop turned and galloped back to the police lines the mob hooting and whooping with delight in his wake. Encouraged, they rushed forward even faster, brandishing their weapons and their flags.

'Charge!' yelled Dunlop at the waiting police. 'Seize their flags and banners! *They must not get through!*'

Albert, carried forward with the surge of navy blue, swerved to the right and aimed for the largest banner which demanded NO COERCION!. He reached up to grab one of the poles but as he pulled it fell towards him, knocking off his helmet.

The battle was soon raging around him. His colleagues, hitting out wildly with their truncheons and fists, were also taking punishment in return. He saw a knife heading for a comrade's back and tried to shout a warning but, at that moment, he was tackled from behind. He turned to fight off the assailant but PC Mc Cullough had already brought his truncheon down on the man's shoulder and he screamed and fell, as did the officer with the knife in his back.

Albert turned in a fury to grab and strike out at the person holding the banner pole. As he caught hold of them he saw a feathered hat falling away from a mass of curly, brown hair, held on only by hat pins, and swaying, ruby-red earrings.

It was a woman! The sight stayed his upraised arm. To hit a woman?

The sun in his eyes made blocked out the upraised hand of the man behind her. The very last thing Albert saw was the iron bar as it came towards his head.

While Best made his way along Whitehall to report to Commissioner Warren, two more squadrons of Life Guards wheeled out of Horse Guards. One was headed for Trafalgar square, the other for Parliament Square. Clearly, he must have been correct in his assumption that the two mobs intended to confront police simultaneously at Westminster Bridge. clearly reinforcements had been called in.

By the time he reached Charing Cross the noise, a bedlam of yells, screams, shouted orders, oaths and trampling feet alerted him to what lay ahead. But on reaching Trafalgar Square, the dead centre of London, the heart of the country and therefore of the Empire, he couldn't believe his eyes.

Chaos reigned. Overlooked by the disdainful King Charles and the heroic Lord Nelson, police and citizens were battling for supremacy. Fighting was hand to hand, no holds barred: truncheons, sticks, stones, fists were all flying. Each side was determined to have its way. The citizens were desperate assert their rights by getting through to the centre at all costs; the police equally desperate to keep them out, make them obey the ban, uphold the law and to succeed against those who had denigrated them.

It was chaos, it was bedlam.

No, Best thought, it was war. Civil war!

To his astonishment the trotting, two-hundred-strong squadron of Life Guards, all scarlet tunics, glittering helmets and breast plates and glinting upright swords, failed to stop to help the beleaguered police but turned left along the south side and galloped off along Cockspur Street towards Waterloo Place.

He knew that the battle was still raging strongly in that quarter but why repulse the mob on that front while the real target was about to be surrendered? How could the old soldier Warren make such an elementary mistake?

At that moment, the fading sun caught the edges of fixed bayonets against a moving backdrop of black bearskins as a column of Grenadier Guards marched into the north west corner of the square and along in front of the National Gallery.

Faced with bayonets the crowd began retreating to the pavement. The soldiers quickly formed a cordon between them and the weary and battered constabulary allowing some police to peel off and reinforce the square's south side. Maybe Warren wasn't such a fool after all.

The mob made plain their bitterness and frustration at this calling in of the troops.

'We could have beaten you lot!' they shouted over their heads at the police. 'You bloody cowards!'

Best's eye was suddenly drawn to a familiar figure among the onlookers; tall and spare with unruly red hair and beard. At first he couldn't quite place this nervous and uncertain figure. Then it dawned. It was the Irishman Bernard Shaw whom he had seen making fiery speeches on street corners and on the platform at Fabian and Socialist Meetings. He didn't look so fiery now: bewildered and frightened more like.

The arrival of the Guards marked the beginning of the end. By 6.20pm the crowds had begun to drift away, some breaking windows where they could as they went and leaving an appalling mess behind: sticks, stones, iron bars, bricks, crushed green rosettes, red flags of all sizes and rotten fruit and vegetables.

Sticking to the urine-and-manure-soaked ground were remnants of the green SDF posters announcing today's meeting, Warren's posters forbidding it and the torn and trampled pages of the socialist newspapers, *Freedom* and *Justice*.

Piled in forlorn heaps: the tattered and torn captured flags and banners proclaiming: **Disobedience to Tyrants is a Duty to God; Put Your Trust in God and Keep Your Powder Dry** and the SDF slogan: **Educate! Agitate! Organise!**

These were soon picked up by a posse of police who formed a column and marched off with them over their shoulders almost like a victorious army. Such triumphalism was a little unnecessary, Best thought.

He sat wearily on the central steps unable to believe it really was all over. His immense relief was tempered by sadness and sympathy for the defeated army of unemployed and sweated labourers. Their cause was mostly a just one but so often sullied by their own rougher elements and betrayed by the faulty judgement of their political leaders.

How stupid to fight over meeting in Trafalgar Square and defy the law when there were much more important battles to be won. No-one stopped them meeting in Hyde Park.

He knew that Trafalgar Square was a more potent and frightening venue for the ruling classes being so close to the seat of government, Buckingham Palace and the gilded gentlemen's clubs of St James's. Meetings there pushed the plight of the poor in the faces of the powerful and the privileged and brought the possibility of revolution up close.

But he could not help feeling immensely relieved that this long, awful day was over at last and that, despite all the fears and warnings, there had been no revolution – yet.

31

They were a sorry lot, thought Best, as he looked at the policemen and their charges lining up outside the court room at Bow Street on the morning after the Battle of Trafalgar Square: bruised, bandaged and limping.

He had seen the immediate aftermath at the Charing Cross Hospital the previous evening.

The scene had been bloodier there, the wounds of the rioters and policemen not yet treated. Cuts and bruises, head injuries from police batons and rioters weapons'; black eyes and broken noses from flailing fists and, particularly in the case of the police casualties; bites on their fingers.

Best had gone there to check on his comrades, especially Albert who was beginning to seem like a son to him, in case the lad's indecision had led him to become a casualty. But there was no sign of him among the wounded which, in one way, was a disappointment. He had news for him. He was going to be listed in Police Orders for having made a Good Arrest and, in addition, Best had submitted a report recommending he be considered for employment as a detective.

'There's more of the police injured over at St Thomas's,' said a uniform sergeant who was nursing a broken arm and a fat lip. 'Those from Parliament Square.'

The two hospitals could scarcely have been more conveniently placed to receive the wounded. The Charing Cross was tucked away behind Trafalgar Square just off the west end of the Strand while St Thomas's sat on the South Bank of the Thames facing the Houses of Parliament.

Best shook his head. 'No. He won't be there. Albert Roberts was in Trafalgar Square. I saw him there myself, twice.'

Back home he had been startled to find a distraught and tearful Helen. A succession of refugees had kept her informed about the raging battle and the many casualties on both sides and, eventually, even the news of the stabbed officer on Westminster Bridge had filtered through. All she could think of was that was where her husband had been heading with the South London march.

Her thoughts had gone around and around the subject until she had become convinced that it had been Best who had been stabbed in the back when a fellow marcher had discovered that he was a police spy. That had set her off reliving the night of the Princess Alice disaster and imagining that their luck could not possibly hold out twice.

Even with his bandaged hands, torn shirt and distracted air, Best's prisoner, Joseph Paxton, looked less battered than some of the others parading for their moment in court. And, unlike most of them, he even seemed serene. Relieved, at having been caught at last. A not uncommon reaction with murderers, even ones like him, who appeared to have lost their hold on reality.

Paxton was mostly silent but when he did speak it all came out in a rush, some of it made sense, some didn't being gibberish. Best was aware that he might be shamming in the hope of being found unfit to plead due to his mental state.

But Best had dealt with many a nutter during his service as all policemen did and felt that Paxton was now the genuine article. He would be sent to an asylum for the criminally insane where at least he would get a bed and food and have no more financial worries.

Best took out his watch. Where was Albert? It was almost ten o'clock. Time for the list to begin. He should be here. After all, this was his arrest. It wasn't like him to be late. Had he made a mistake in recommending him? Was the lad not yet ready to take on the responsibilities of a detective?

There was a commotion behind them as burly Constable McCullough, who had a swollen mouth and one front tooth missing, joined the queue. As he did so he propelled ahead of him an equally burly gentleman with a large bandage around his right ear.

'Shame about Albert,' he said to Best as he settled in.

Best frowned. 'What do you mean?'

'Knocked unconscious on Westminster Bridge. That South London mob. Ferocious they were. He's in St Thomas's. It's bad they say.'

'But he was in *Trafalgar Square*,' Best insisted doggedly.

McCullough shook his head then winced at the movement.

'Nah. They moved him up to Parliament Square. Heard there was going to be an ambush so they rushed some of us up there.'

St Thomas's Hospital had been called ancient in 1215 but its' eight elegant pavilions flanking the south side of the Thames looked as if they had only been built yesterday which, of course, they had.

As a rookie policeman Best had been part of the ceremonial guard when Queen Victoria opened the new hospital sixteen years earlier. Now he hastened to the entrance watched impassively by her fully-robed seated majesty wrought in marble.

Albert's condition, he had been told, remained critical. There was little hope.

He knew it was ridiculous to blame himself for the fact that Albert had ended up at Westminster Bridge to greet the South and West London marches but if it hadn't been for his conclusions about an intended ambush he would not have been sent there.

As he hurried down one of the corridors linking the pavilions he could not help replaying the sequence of events and wondering whether something he had said or done could have been said or done differently? Perhaps he should not have been so convincing about the huge numbers involved? But then, there had been huge numbers and huge numbers had been required to repulse them – and he was being ridiculous.

Perhaps if he had seen Albert quick marching towards his fate he could have insisted he needed his assistance on some task – or at least managed to tell him that his desired goal of becoming a detective was within his reach at last.

Now he was being stupid. Trying to rearrange the past. He wished Helen was here so she could talk some sense into him – and share his anguish. It felt like Joseph all over again.

It was outside the strict visiting hours but in this instance they would be relaxed just a little he was informed by one of the pristine nurses who crackled towards him in her starched uniform.

Nonetheless, he would have to wait until they judged Albert ready to receive him. How ready would he have to be if he was unconscious, Best wondered? Ridiculous. But the St Thomas's nurses were Florence Nightingale trained and would brook no dissent.

He had been waiting on a bench in the ward corridor for almost ten minutes, lost in his own melancholy thoughts, when he became aware of quiet sobbing close by.

He turned around to see a young woman sitting alongside him. Judging by the bruising around her neck and cheeks and swelling under her right eye she too was one of yesterday's casualties. Either that or her husband had given her a beating. Then he took in the rest of her features and her Salvation Army uniform.

'Good God – it's Florence!' he exclaimed. 'What on earth *happened* to you?'

'Stark came for me.'

Best was horrified.

Between sobs she explained that Stark had attacked her in the stairwell of number 17, Rye Court and begun dragging her down to the cellars.

'But Joe Benbow saved me. I had told him he didn't need to see me out but Elsa got worried and made him come after me – and,' she sobbed, 'he saved my life. But what's the use of a life without Albert!'

'Where is Stark now?'

'In prison.'

'Nobody told *me*,' Best exclaimed then realised they would not have been able to reach him. He had been on the march, then in Trafalgar Square and then at court with Paxton. There would be a message waiting for him at the Yard.

'They are taking him to court tomorrow. I have to be there.'

'Me too,' said Best.

32

Best could not believe this madness was continuing. He tried to concentrate on the faces as man after man climbed into the witness box at Marlborough Street Magistrate's Court, swore their allegiance to the Queen and promised that they were prepared to help uphold her peace and quell disorder.

Some were top-hatted gentlemen of means obviously out to protect their property and have a little fun while doing it. The others were ex Army and Navy Officers, bankers, solicitors, accountants, merchants, shop assistants, clerks, ushers and messengers. Quite a number were of uncertain provenance.

In response to a call for Special Constables to protect the populace from the rabble thousands had come forward. So, they had got the quantity they had asked for but the quality of these volunteers was now worrying the authorities. Which was why Best and his fellow detectives were obliged to attend various London Courts to weed out 'objectionable characters'.

In other words, they were searching for familiar faces belonging to those likely to be delighted with this opportunity to do a bit of thieving under the protection of the striped armband of the Metropolitan Police Special Constabulary and trouble-making Anarchists or socialists keen on acting as fifth columnists.

Various volunteer corps had also offered their services en masse including, Best was surprised to learn, The London Irish.

The Special Constables were required to assist police in ensuring there were no more invasions of Trafalgar Square particularly on the coming Sunday. Also, to free some policemen so they could return to their beats in the suburbs where the unguarded populace now feared for their lives and property.

It had not been forgotten that it was such a mass enrolment of a Special Constabulary which had helped ensure the defeat of the reformist group, the Chartists, back in 1848 when the newly-fashioned square had just been opened to the public.

Best's thoughts kept going back to Albert, who lay unmoving in his bed at St Thomas's. 'No change,' was the message the ward sister and nurses kept chanting.

Well trained as they were neither they nor the doctors could give any indication whether there *ever* would be any change. But he knew by their guarded words and expressions that it was unlikely. Despite the heavy blow he had suffered there was no evidence of any skull fracture but, they pointed out, brain swelling or internal bleeding could lead to death at any moment and often did.

One week after Bloody Sunday, as that day had been dubbed by *The Pall Mall Gazette*, Trafalgar Square was packed with police and specials but despite threats to the contrary, few socialist, radicals or anarchists. They were holding an 'indignation meeting' in Hyde Park. Afterwards, however, many of them just happened to be passing the square as were many more eager spectators.

When these crowds began to thicken the police and specials pushed them back. In the melee one young man, Alfred Linnell, a radical lawyer, was trampled by a police horse – just as a policeman had been on Bloody Sunday. But Linnell, who suffered a fractured femur, died.

It was said that the numbers in Linnell's funeral procession exceeded those at that of the massively popular Duke of Wellington in 1852. The graveside oration was given by William Morris who also composed a Death Song in Linnell's honour.

Ten days after Bloody Sunday, Joseph Paxton was found to be unfit to plead and sent to Broadmoor Criminal Lunatic Asylum and Stark, admitting nothing and showing no remorse, was committed to the Central Criminal Court for trial.

Two weeks after Bloody Sunday Best again took tea with Mrs Myers but this time declined the Madeira Cake in favour of delicious coconut macaroons. Sticky, but more worth the effort.

There was something on his mind. Some unfinished business. He did not *need* to know the answer, since the murderer had been caught and dealt with, but he wanted to solve the one remaining puzzle.

He had the foolish idea, superstition even, that as Albert had solved the first one, he should find the answer to this one. Then he could tell Albert 'when he woke up' and that, somehow it would help ensure that he did.

'Mrs Myers,' he said wiping the sugary substance from his fingers with a lacy napkin, 'would you mind satisfying my idle curiosity?'

'Of course not, Earnest, she smiled at him, 'and call me Adeline, please.'

'Adeline,' he said, 'in your husband's diary was an entry which said,' "Decide whether to leave." Or something like that..'

He paused, still wondering whether he was doing the right thing. Was he being insensitive? Oh, well, it was too late now. 'Do you know what he was referring to? Was he contemplating leaving a club or the SDF or . . .'

She shook her head sadly. 'We were trying to make up our minds whether to leave Hackney. Move further west nearer some of my relatives and the SDF offices. We were torn because it would mean a longer journey to work for Andrew. That being so, I left the final decision to him. I have to admit I did hope it might help persuade him to give up working at the dock. That used to upset him so much you know. All that misery and hardship.' A tear sprung into her eye. 'But he will never know that now, will he.'

Something simple, that was what he had told Albert, and so it was. He should listen to his own advice.

Three weeks after the Bloody Sunday riot Stark was convicted and sentenced to death. Two days later Albert opened his eyes. When he regained his senses properly he remembered nothing of the fracas which had overwhelmed him and little of Bloody Sunday.

'You hesitated,' Best teased him but when the lad looked crestfallen added, 'for the best of reasons. You were reluctant to strike a woman. Florence is very proud of you, Detective Constable, Third Class.'

Albert grinned happily and fingered his still purple bruises. 'Not one of Warren's Wolves any more then?'

'Oh, I wouldn't say that,' said Best.

Author's Notes

The background events and several of the characters in *Dead Centre* are real. The years following 1887 also proved turbulent:

1888 Jack the Ripper Murders
The Match Girls' Strike.
1889 The Great London Dock Strike
1890 The Metropolitan Police Strike.

Criticism over the handling of the **Jack the Ripper** murders and the lack of support he received from the Home Office, finally induced Commissioner of Police **Charles Warren** to resign. Senior officers were sorry to lose him. However, a constable (responding to Warren's article outlining his complaints) claimed that they were fed up with having to control and suppress working class demonstrations with which they were in sympathy. In recent times Warren's role has been re-examined and he is now seen as one of the better, if unluckiest, of Commissioners.

    Annie Besant, (Fabian and lover of the young George Bernard Shaw) led The Match Girl's Strike which won better pay and conditions for workers. She later went to live in India and became involved with the Indian nationalist movement.

    Henry Champion and SDF members including **John Burns** were active in the Great London Dock Strike of 1889 which won dock labourers their 'dockers tanner' (sixpence an hour) and better working conditions although the calling on system remained until the mid twentieth century. The strike was saved from defeat by the extraordinary generosity of the Australian Labour movement who donated £30,000 to the strike relief fund.

That year Burns, too, left the SDF after a disagreement with Hyndman. In 1892 John Burns became Liberal MP for Battersea and, in 1906, the first working man to achieve cabinet office although many of his old comrades felt that during his time in office he let the socialist movement down.

The Police Act of 1890 failed to address the questions of low pay and the desire for a union or negotiating body. When 130 men refused to go on duty at Bow Street the Commissioner (Colonel Sir Edward Bradford) sacked 39 ringleaders and transferred others. The strike fizzled out but the grievances did not. More widespread and serious police strikes in 1918 and 1919 led to the formation of the Police Federation but not of a union although the need for one was mooted again only recently.

Improvements in the economy boosted employment and a lessened the enthusiasm for demonstrations.

William Morris became pessimistic about the likelihood of a popular civil rising. He resigned from Socialist League, as did several other members, and the League petered out. The SDF continued activities until 1911 when the Independent Labour Party (formed 1893) absorbed many floating socialists.

H H Champion went to live in Australia where he established the Fabian movement. Gough Whitlam and Bob Hawkes later became members. But Champion upset the local unions with his damaging criticisms of the handling of their Maritime Strike.

H M Hyndman exchanged his silk topper for a soft hat and became involved with the emerging Independent Labour Party. But many members were uncomfortable with his Marxism and in 1911 he established the British Socialist Party which failed to win any Parliamentary seats.

George Bernard Shaw, who had been tempted to become a member of the SDF but chose the Fabians because they appeared more educated, later revealed that the character of Tanner, in his play, *Man and Superman*, was a pen portrait of the external Hyndman. He claimed that Hyndman and Morris had let the movement go to pieces by playing at soldiers with it and the reason they didn't get on was that they were both sons of wealthy parents and so had all the petulance which this exceptional condition produced in strong personalities.

The ban on meetings in Trafalgar Square was lifted in 1892. Since then, it has been the scene of countless rowdy meetings and riots although lately is being used for more celebratory events particularly those involving ethnic minorities.

Foreign observers noticed the prominent role of Trafalgar Square in British life. Adolf Hitler's invasion plan included a suggestion that they should dismantle Nelson's column and transfer it to Berlin to bring home the fact that they now ruled the waves and everything else as well.

Those wishing to learn more about the 'dead centre' of London will find a good source – and one I wish I had discovered earlier - in the recently reissued, *Trafalgar Square: Emblem of Empire,* by Rodney Mace (Lawrence & Wishart, 2005).

Made in the USA
Charleston, SC
22 September 2016